M M

A Candlelight Ecstasy Romance ®

"YOU STUPID IDIOT! YOU COULD HAVE BEEN KILLED PULLING A STUNT LIKE THAT!"

Suddenly all the fears of the past day washed over Robin. Anger and hatred warred through her mind. "Don't you think I know that now?" she raged. "When I came back later and saw you holding that knife like you wanted to—"

"What?"

Furiously, Robin struggled free of his hold. She pushed his strong hands away angrily, her eyes snapping. "Go away! I don't want to talk to you anymore!"

"Look," Nick said. "You have to tell me what happened. I don't remember any of this."

"No! Go away! Just leave me alone!"

Nick stood first, then leaned over, hauling Robin to her feet and then high into his arms. He carried her back to the couch in the front room. She lay in his embrace, her arms around his neck, unable to understand her burning need for this stranger who had violated her refuge and made her a prisoner of love. . . .

A CANDLELIGHT ECSTASY ROMANCE ®

A NIGHT
IN THE
FOREST

Alysse Rasmussen

A CANDLELIGHT ECSTASY ROMANCE ®

Published by
Dell Publishing Co., Inc.
1 Dag Hammarskjold Plaza
New York, New York 10017

Dell ® TM 681510, Dell Publishing Co., Inc.
Candlelight Ecstasy Romance®, 1,203,540, is a registered
trademark of Dell Publishing Co., Inc.,
New York, New York.

ISBN: 0-440-16399-4

Printed in the United States of America
First printing—March 1984

To my Ex-Master Peon,
Ellen Chaffee—you see, I
didn't forget, did I?—and
to anyone else who has
been crazy(?) enough to
enjoy working the graveyard shift.

To Our Readers:

We have been delighted with your enthusiastic response to Candlelight Ecstasy Romances®, and we thank you for the interest you have shown in this exciting series.

In the upcoming months we will continue to present the distinctive sensuous love stories you have come to expect only from Ecstasy. We look forward to bringing you many more books from your favorite authors and also the very finest work from new authors of contemporary romantic fiction.

As always, we are striving to present the unique, absorbing love stories that you enjoy most—books that are more than ordinary romance.

Your suggestions and comments are always welcome. Please write to us at the address below.

Sincerely,

The Editors
Candlelight Romances
1 Dag Hammarskjold Plaza
New York, New York 10017

CHAPTER ONE

"And next on KOSI, an old favorite, John Denver's 'Rocky Mountain High.'"

The radio announcer's voice faded as the melodic strains and the beautiful lyrics of the popular song poured forth from the stereo. As the last notes faded softly away, Robin lifted her eyes from the sketch pad she had been using.

That song always brought tears to her eyes. The idea of finding a haven away from the rat race of the rest of the world made her think of her own family's situation and the peace that they had found underneath these glorious Rocky Mountain skies. Although not normally a religiose person, here in the splendor of the cathedrallike mountains, Robin felt that God was closer, more real, almost tangible.

The craggy peaks that towered over the low valley guarded it, protected it. The valley was also a sanctuary. Nature's sanctuary. It echoed the powerful mountain in its own soft and gentle manner, protecting the needy.

Robin noticed a white streak pass outside the floor-to-ceiling windows of the dining room. A large rabbit, plump and furry, hopped across the snow. It moved cautiously but showed no real fear. It knew instinctively that it was safe and secure in the peaceful valley.

Robin smiled, understanding and sharing in the rabbit's security. As a small child her family had visited the valley each year. Her father had often said that the time he spent in the valley was the only thing that enabled him to face the rest of the year in the busy city where they had lived almost one thousand miles to the east. When her father became successful as an architect, he and her mother had placed a down payment on the land in the valley. Years later, on the Fourth of July, they had made a huge production of burning the paid mortgage papers.

Robin remembered fondly the times they had spent living in tents because her father, well-known architect that he was, had not been able to design a house that would blend with perfection to the glory of the mountains and the splendor of the forests. Even though Lewis Peters had purchased the legal right to do with the land anything he wished, he felt compelled to leave the land in peace.

Later when Robin's family moved to the valley permanently they had been rewarded a thousand times over for leaving most of the land to nature's way. The valley had repaid them with the solace that they needed. Her parents had protected the valley from invasions of man and machinery, from developers and exploiters. Now the valley protected them, offering her parents and herself its comfort.

After the tragic accident that had left her mother crippled and in a wheelchair, Robin and her parents had been drawn, compelled even, to return to the valley. Robin remembered the morning when her father had come bursting into the hospital room where her mother lay recuperating after yet another operation that had failed, due to a lack of sensitive medical equipment. The only comfort he could offer Robin's mother was that he had finally designed a house that would bring them the peace they so desperately needed.

Robin looked around her now. The house was a nature lover's dream, as it was built around a square courtyard of snow-covered lawn and lacy birch. A hallway of slate tile was enclosed by full-length windows that overlooked the courtyard. The other rooms of the house all opened off the encompassing hall. There were very few walls, most of which were especially designed to conduct solar energy. The house, designed with her mother in mind, was all on one level with the exception of the sunken living room that had three steps and, on two sides, ramps of black slate. Full-length windows peaked to form a cathedral ceiling that ran from the living room all the way around the entire southern portion of the house to end dramatically with an indoor garden area just east of the modern kitchen.

Lewis, knowing the love his wife had for all things green and growing, had set the garden between the open kitchen and dining room. It held the usual kitchen-garden variety of herbs and vegetables as well as a number of flowers and grasses. Throughout the rest of the house potted plants, ferns, and small trees repeated the garden theme.

Robin's gaze roamed the snow-covered forest and moved to the grandeur of the mountains. Impressed yet again by their breathtaking beauty, their peaceful tranquility, their rugged protection, she reached for her pencil and sketch pad, trying to express her feelings in bold geometric lines.

Adding one last stroke, Robin held the design up in front of her. Her small hands turned it this way and that. She studied it critically, not completely satisfied, but acknowledged that it was better than previous attempts. She glanced ruefully around the mountain valley, knowing

11

what she felt, wanting to be able to express it, share it, yet, as always, the combination of towering mountains and gentle valley remained an elusive quality.

Still, her newest design did manage to express the power of the mountain. Robin raked slender fingers through her long brown hair, yawned tiredly, and began to make the alterations that would enhance the rugged majesty of the mountains. Adding one last decisive stroke, she sat back satisfied, knowing that this design—Cathedral Mountain —would make a fantastic quilt.

Her stomach rumbled. A glance at the mantelpiece revealed that it was after two o'clock in the afternoon. Was it really so late? She patted the protesting region of her anatomy solicitously. It had every right to complain, for she had been sitting at the dining room table working on her designs since six o'clock that morning.

Cramped muscles protested when Robin stood up. She ignored their complaining and smiled with self-indulgent pleasure at the sheaf of designs she had completed. When she started sewing, designing, and planning her projects she lost all track of time. And that wasn't a bad thing.

Robin frowned. Worry over her mother niggled at her brain. Ever since the accident six years ago, Margaret Peters had been very delicate. She had spent two years in and out of hospitals undergoing numerous operations; but they had all been unsuccessful. For the past four years Robin and her parents had been living in the mountains near Rifle, Colorado. Now for the first time in years, her parents had gone back to see a specialist in St. Louis, because her mother had been experiencing some unusual pains.

They had asked her to accompany them, but she had elected to stay at home. She had commitments to teach various aspects of handicrafts to several local church groups, as well as to judge numerous local and regional

12

shows in quilting, embroidery, and other needlework arts. To leave would have been unfair to her students and friends.

Nonetheless, Robin was terribly worried about her mother. If these recurring pains indicated a worsening of her mother's general condition . . .

The telephone pealed insistently, stridently demanding Robin's attention. She walked from the sunken front room along the wide, open hall and into the study where she answered the telephone. Mindful of possible business contacts for either herself or her father, Robin answered it in a professional and businesslike manner.

The voice at the other end was deep and masculine. "Robin, this is Daddy. How are you, Babe?"

Robin wrinkled her nose. Her father would never see her as a full-grown adult.

"Fine." She answered mildly, not willing, for once, to engage in their usual verbal sparring over the hated pet name. All her concern was with her mother and the results of the week-long testing. "How's Mom?"

"She's fine, Babe. Honest. But I'm afraid that I have some bad news for you. Your mother and I won't be able to make it home for Thanksgiving. And I doubt that we will make it home for Christmas either."

Anxiety brought tears to Robin's eyes. "Dad, what's wrong? Why won't you be home?"

"It's your mother, Robin. I don't know how to tell you this, but . . ." His voice began to wobble.

Robin clutched the receiver tightly. Her knuckles shone whitely through the flesh of her hands. She swayed with shock. Fear gripped icily at her throat. Her breath came in short, sharp, pain-filled gasps. *Not her mother! Not her beautiful, vital mother!*

Robin's consciousness barely registered the prolonged fumbling on the other end of the line. She was too busy fighting to control the tears that crowded her eyes. The muscles in her throat cramped tightly, dreading to ask what was wrong, fearing the answer.

"Lewis, give me that phone!" Her mother's clear, sweet tones came from a great distance. "You've probably scared Robin half to death. Men!" The disgusted word was spat forcefully across the wires.

"Robin, darling! Don't cry, love. I'm fine! I swear it. What your father was so ineptly trying to tell you is that far from being worse, I'm showing signs of improvement."

Robin could barely take it in. "Improvement?"

Margaret laughed like a young girl. Carefree. Pleased. Excited. "Well, something like that. The pains were just acting as signals, letting me and the doctors know that the nerves were still somewhat functional. But actually, it's the medical situation that has improved the most."

"Mother," begged Robin. "What are you talking about?"

Margaret spoke quickly. "While I was here, Andrew McCauley, you remember him don't you?"

Robin immediately brought to mind a picture of the tall, white-haired physician who had operated on her mother so many times. "Yes, I remember him."

"Well," Margaret continued, "Andrew referred me to this brilliant young surgeon. He said the young man was, and I quote, dynamite in his field. His name is Santos, Paulo Santos.

"Oh, Robin," she continued with a quickly drawn breath. "He became interested in spinal problems like mine while he was still studying medicine in Chicago. And now there is some new equipment—well, it isn't all that new, but it combines some ideas from micro and laser surgery and can be used more successfully in cases like mine. I'll let your father tell you more about it later.

14

Darling, can you believe it?" Margaret's voice crackled with happiness. "When I come home I may be walking."

The tears dried on Robin's cheeks. Hope filled her face, making it radiant with joy. "Walking?" Her voice was low and hushed, reluctant to let out that magic word for fear that it would take fright and run away. "Really walking?"

Her mother continued excitedly. "Yes, darling, *really* walking! Dr. Santos says that I have an eighty-five percent chance."

"Eighty-five percent? Oh, Mother, are they really that sure? I can't believe it. I'm so happy for you and for Daddy and for me. I just can't believe it."

"I know, darling. I could hardly believe it myself at first."

The two women chatted on at some length, the older woman telling her daughter about the operation that would take place in just a few day's time. The preliminary results would not be known until after Thanksgiving. If the operation was successful, it would be well after the first of the year before Margaret and Lewis would be able to return home.

"It sounds wonderful." Robin's voice held just a trace of a wobble. "I've missed you terribly, and I was so worried."

"I know, darling," Margaret's words were soft and loving. She understood her daughter very well. "That's why we called so early in the day. I wanted to tell you the news so that you would stop worrying about my being worse rather than better."

Her mother's reference to time caused Robin to take an automatic glance at the desk clock. "Mother! Look at the time! We've been talking on the phone for over and hour and a half—and in the middle of a weekday too. I didn't stop to think. This must be costing Daddy a fortune!"

"We were just so excited we couldn't wait until this

evening to let you know," Margaret explained with an unusual disregard of extravagance.

"I'm so glad you didn't wait." Robin's reply was choked.

"Will you be all right, darling?" Margaret asked, forever a mother, with a mother's concerns.

"I'll be fine, Mom." Robin assured her mother. "When we finish I am going to hang up, sit down, and have a good howl just out of sheer happiness and relief. And then—oh, I don't know—I'll think of something to do."

Her mother laughed. "I know the feeling. I have this incredible urge to get up and do a jig right now, but I guess it'll have to wait a few more months. Any message that you would like me to give to your father?"

"Just tell Daddy that I love him." Robin began to laugh, her spirits soaring high. The exhilaration was irrepressible. "And you can tell him that I l-o-a-t-h-e"—Robin drawled the word out—"being called *Babe.*"

Her mother was laughingly passing on the message when the connection was finally severed.

When Thanksgiving arrived Robin was alone in her home amid the Rockies. Her last class had ended the night before. The students had put on a small quilt show, demonstrating the finished products and the skills they had acquired during the ten-week quilting session. Robin had acted as the judge, awarding prizes for best overall construction, best use of fabric, and best quilting technique. It had been a gay occasion, with everyone infected by the holiday atmosphere.

Today seemed doubly lonely in comparison. Robin sighed, getting up to switch off the Thanksgiving Day parade, which was being aired live from New York City. Somehow she just didn't feel in the mood to celebrate.

Robin walked up the three short steps to the raised

hallway and headed toward the kitchen at the far end of the house. Opening the refrigerator door she grimaced at the contents. Robin reached for the makings of a salad and some leftover chicken. Not at all her family's usual Thanksgiving Day fare. The meal was hurriedly assembled and speedily dispatched. Robin felt bored and restless. She knew that she was missing her parents and that they would be calling later that evening, but it did not help to make the morning and afternoon go any faster.

After the dishes had been washed and dried and put away, Robin wandered down the back hall, stopping to straighten the bathroom for a moment before wandering into her parents' bedroom. It was large, almost eighteen by eighteen feet. A huge king-size bed dominated the room and was covered by a colorful postage-stamp quilt.

Robin viewed the quilt with pride. It had been an enormous undertaking and not just because of its size. Each half inch square piece had been carefully cut by hand, so that Robin had actually been able to design a replica of a stained glass window, faithfully depicting the scene of the Crucifixion.

And when it was finished, Robin had offered it as partial fulfillment for her Master of Arts and had later submitted it in a national quilting competition, where it had taken first place in the patchwork quilt division. Although the prize money had just barely covered the cost of the fabric, the prestige of winning had been its own reward. An additional bonus had come when Robin had been approached by one of the leading design houses in the handicraft industry and asked to submit some of her designs for consideration. That, in turn, had lead to her being offered a permanent position on their staff.

Later, after her mother's accident, Robin had turned down the position of head designer at Quiltique with only a minimal amount of regret. Instead, she had elected to work as a freelance designer for any number of houses, seeing it as the perfect solution, since it would enable her to return to the valley and help her parents, especially her mother, without either of them knowing just how promising a career opportunity she was turning down.

Yet, wanting to return and help her parents had not been as selfless as it had seemed, and Robin was the first to admit it, for while she truly adored her parents, another major factor had been the actual mountains and the valley. So by accepting freelance commissions only, Robin had been able to work in a field that had satisfied her artistic and creative nature as well as providing her with the opportunity of living in the heart of the Rocky Mountains. And it was proving to be lucrative too. Almost everything she designed had been accepted by one handicraft house or another.

Robin stroked the intricate postage-stamp quilt, enjoying the feel of its uneven texture beneath her fingers. The new design she had started a few days ago, the Cathedral Mountain quilt, was ready to be cut. Perhaps if she started it now, time would not hang so heavily on her hands.

Leaving her parents' room, Robin walked swiftly past her own room and went into the study cum workroom. She hummed a popular tune of John Denver's while she searched through the built-in cedar cabinets for just the right pieces of fabric for her new project. Having selected a number of strong, true cottons, Robin headed for the dining room.

Since the quilt design had already been graphed out to scale, it only took a few seconds for Robin to choose the proper size plastic templates. She spent the rest of the afternoon and early evening tracing around the templates and cutting out the small pieces of material on the dining room table. Once the pieces had been cut, she strung them together on a line of thread. When the telephone rang, Robin had just finished stringing the last piece of fabric.

Knowing that the call would be from her parents, Robin answered casually. "Hello?"

Her father's voice filled the earpiece of the reciever booming across the lines from St. Louis to their home in the mountains just a few miles northeast of Rifle. "Babe, how are you? We have some great news. We won't be home for Christmas after all."

Robin began laughing. "That *is* great news. I didn't want you back anyway. And I *hate* being called Babe."

Her father's response was perfunctory. "Sorry, Robin, I forgot."

"You always forget." She moaned in mock exasperation. Then she asked more soberly. "Is it really true? You won't be home for Christmas? And Mother will be able to walk again?"

"Yes, Babe, your mother will come home walking." Her father's voice was filled with joyful reassurance. "She will have to have one more operation and then until the muscles build themselves up again she will still need to use the wheelchair. Gradually she'll advance to walkers and eventually to a cane. After that, no one can tell yet, but it might even mean a complete recovery."

"Oh, Daddy, I'm so happy. It's like a dream come true."

. They chatted on for a few minutes more, then her father relinquished the telephone to his wife. After another prolonged conversation concerning Margaret's progress, her parents said good-bye and broke the connection.

Robin wandered back into the dining room feeling happier than she had been in years. She tidied up her materials and put her tools away. Tomorrow she would start sewing on the quilt; she was too keyed up to do any more on it tonight. As for now, she would go for a walk in the forest.

She fixed herself another hurried meal and ate it quickly. Then she pulled on heavy boots and a down parka and, still tugging on her mittens, she let herself out the kitchen's sliding glass door. The snow was already deep this year and it had only just begun. Kicking up puffs of the fine powdery substance, Robin estimated that there was probably close to four inches on the ground before heading into the forest that surrounded her home.

The trees of pine and fir inched their way slowly down the sides of the mountains. Their greenness was occasionally highlighted by a glimpse of the bare bark of cottonwood, aspen, and birch. When she reached a particularly advantageous outcropping, she turned and studied the valley below. This was her home. It had been so since she had returned to help care for her mother four years ago. Now that her mother would no longer need her help, there would be no obstacles in Robin's path. She could leave this place if she chose to do so. She could go anywhere in the world. She could do anything. At twenty-nine, with a successful career to her credit, she was once again completely in charge of her own life and answerable to no one.

Studying the landscape around her, Robin admitted to herself that there was no place else she would rather be. She had wanted to come home after her husband Randy had died, but she had known that she needed to establish a life for herself that was separate from her family. Yet, when her mother needed her, she had not hesitated, for she had learned in the months and years that followed Randy's death that she could stand on her own. And now this land had become her land. It held her stronger than any other love or passion. She would willingly give up her career and much, much more to remain here. Perhaps her father would design her a smaller home, a place of her own, down by the lake. Randy would have liked the lake.

A small, wistful smile played at the corners of her

20

mouth. She didn't think about Randy too much anymore —or, rather, when she thought of him, it was not with sadness and pain, but rather with fondness and regret that he had died so young. The plans they had made . . . the dreams they had dreamt . . . they had been young and deeply in love. No more than babes in the woods. Did anyone fall in love like that anymore?

As the snow began to fall softly, Robin turned back toward the trail that led down to the valley. Although her eyes tracked the path, her heart brought a different image to mind: blond hair, blue eyes, laughing lips, and cheeks that never seemed to have more than peach fuzz no matter what the time of day.

CHAPTER TWO

On a Friday, two weeks before Christmas, the late afternoon sun's watery rays made no appreciable attempt to lighten the gloomy interior of the workroom of Armstrong Engineering and Computing Services, Inc. Overhead, a solitary fluorescent light glared, adding no warmth to the room. Even the incandescent light bulb over the drafting table shed no warmth.

The room itself had been cleverly designed and decorated to give the worker a feeling of warmth and security; yet, today, it stubbornly refused to cooperate, leaving its sole occupant feeling cold and disgruntled.

Cold brown muck, doubling for coffee, swirled malevolently in a foam cup that was lifted to the lips of Nicholas Armstrong. He was the only thing that appeared to add warmth and vitality to the sterile atmosphere of the workroom.

Nick grimaced in distaste and returned the bitter brew to its former location. He shifted on his stool and tried to find a more comfortable position, wondering vaguely why he felt so depressed. Normally he looked forward to

Christmas, enjoying the added hustle and bustle, the coldness of the air, and the camaraderie that even perfect strangers seemed to share during the Christmas season.

Leaning back from the drawing table, Nick's eyes focused on the tall buildings visible through the grimy panes of glass. Dismal, dreary edifices of concrete and steel hovered viciously over the equally unpleasant streets below.

"Even the snow is grungy!" Nick muttered in disgust.

"Did you say something, Nick?" Blond ringlets topped the head of the pert blue-eyed woman who popped through the door.

Shaking his hand in a gesture of denial Nick automatically began to assess the shapely curves of the cute plump blonde before him. He eyed her full figure and rounded curves. The cheerful red fabric of her dress pleased his eye. Her round face was alive and glowing.

"Nicholas Armstrong!" Liz scolded, laughter evident in her light, teasing voice. "You should be ashamed of yourself."

"Huh?" Nick pulled his gaze from her figure and focused, puzzled, on the blue eyes of her face. "How come?"

Liz laughed again. Her eyes sparkling she flicked her hand from shoulder to hip. "What would Thomas say?" she teased.

Dull red seeped into Nick's lean cheeks. His apology was sincere. "I am sorry, Liz. Call it force of habit."

"What is a force of habit?" The gravelly voice of Tom Jenkins preceded his burly form.

"I was leering evilly at your wife." Nick replied evenly. The three of them had grown up together. It would have taken more than an appreciative leer to upset their friendship.

Tom moved behind his wife, slipping his arms around

23

her waist. Giving her plump form a tight squeeze and a seductive smile, he applauded his friend's good taste.

"Mmm. She is well worth the look."

Both men automatically and simultaneously appraised her form again. One gaze was clinically detached, the other more personal and involved.

Elizabeth Jenkins, a wife of ten years and the mother of two, blushed. Ignoring her husband, she turned thoughtfully to her boss, who was also the godfather of her children.

"What you need, Nick, is a good woman," she stated forcefully.

"What do I need?" Tom teased, waggling his sandy brows.

Liz laughed. "You need your ears boxed."

"How come Nick gets a good woman and I get my ears boxed?" Tom's expression clearly stated that he found that a gross miscarriage of justice.

"Because you already have a good woman," was her smug reply. Liz patted her husband's cheek fondly before turning back to Nick.

"Seriously, Nick, you need to get rid of that string of long-legged model types you keep company with."

"What's wrong with long-legged model types?" Wry humor glinted in Nick's sharp, cobalt gaze.

"Well," Liz drawled, "for one thing, their bra size is bigger than their IQ's."

Nick just laughed. The reply had not been unexpected.

Tom teased his wife, tongue-in-cheek. "I didn't think they wore bras." One eyebrow arched, inviting Nick's comments.

Nick refrained from entering the scrimmage, while Liz snapped back triumphantly. "If they don't wear them, it's only because the hooks and eyes are too complicated for them to master."

24

When Tom opened his mouth to continue the battle of wits, Nick called out. "*Pax!* Peace! Time out!" Genuine mirth danced in his mobile features. "What would I do without the two of you?"

"What?"

"Huh?"

Two pair of confused eyes looked back into the amused blue ones of their friend. They had momentarily forgotten his presence while engaging in their verbal sparring.

Nick shrugged. "Pre-Christmas blues, I guess. I was staring out of the window, thinking how gray and dismal everything seemed to be, when Liz walked in all bright and cheery."

Nick added mockingly, "Now, this lively and enlightening discussion—I must admit, you're both good for my morale."

"You'll feel better after you see your family, Nick," Tom insisted seriously.

"Mmm. I hope so."

Liz wondered uneasily if Nick's father's new wife was part of the problem. After all, she was only about five or six years older than Nick and he had been squiring her about when . . .

"How are your dad and Jill, anyway?" Tom asked.

Nick's face was free from shadows. His genuine pleasure reassured Liz that Jill was not at the root of his depression.

"They're fine. Terrific, in fact. Dad says he never felt better. Jill is a miracle worker. He's lost twenty pounds and he said she won't let him work on the farm for more than a few hours a day. In fact, the last report from the cardiologist shows that his heart has improved too."

"Great!" chorused the Jenkinses.

Nick sank back into an upholstered chair that stood to

25

one side of the drafting table. His grin of self-indulgent pride was slightly self-deprecatory too.

"I make a great matchmaker, even if I do go out with empty-headed, long-legged model types."

Liz laughingly defended Jill. "Jill was the exception. She may have looked the part, but she never acted it."

"I know." Nick agreed readily, remembering how well Jill and his father had hit it off when he had introduced them last winter. Later Jill had asked him how long his mother had been dead and then, when he had told her that his father had been a widower for over five years, Jill had asked him if his father had ever mentioned the possibility of remarrying. Nick had been forced to say no, but had added that he wished his father would. Even now Jill's response had the power to make him laugh softly to himself. It wasn't every day that your date told you she would rather be your stepmother than your lover. But Jill had done it in a most delightful way.

His manager's next question brought Nicholas out of his daydreams.

"When are you leaving?" Tom asked.

"I have a plane reservation for four o'clock tomorrow afternoon on the commuter flight from O'Hare. I figured I would go to the office party tonight and finish any shopping and packing that I needed to do tomorrow morning. But if I am going to get away on time, I had better get back to work now. I promised Green's that I would send over the preliminary sketches of that new computerized punch press they want to set up. Do you have a copy of the list of specifications that I want to send along with it?"

Liz shook her head. "I think Sandy has it. I'll just go and make sure that it is finished."

"I'll go help you," her husband suggested.

Nick laughed, calling out behind them. "Remember, if

I don't get away on time, you don't get your holiday either."

"Hmm." Tom considered the situation carefully with only his twinkling eyes belying his apparent gravity. "I guess Liz can look for them on her own." Suddenly all business, he added. "Maybe I'll give Henderson's a call. They still haven't submitted the cost estimates for the welding job on Grant's new project."

Nick frowned. "Isn't that the third or fourth time they've been late with their estimates?"

"Yeah. They've been late in completing their contracts too. I hate to do it because they are able to offer some really attractive prices, but I think we had better find a new welding firm for our work."

"Better talk it over with Grant first, then go ahead. But see if you can get Grant to suggest it. That way he won't feel so bad about it. I know he suggested changing to Henderson's in the first place, and if they had done as they promised, it would have been quite a coup for our budding, young industrial intern. If he suggests the change, I think it would be better; that way he won't feel like he failed on a portion of his training."

Tom grinned. "That boy is going places."

Nick agreed. "He's good, Tom. Almost as good as you are."

"Whoops! I'd better look to my laurels." Tom waved and disappeared around the corner, already trying to formulate how he could encourage their young student-intern, Grant Ziegler, from the University of Platteville's industrial technology program to suggest changing welding companies for his latest project.

Nick was about five minutes late when he and his date arrived at the Khyber of India. He hastily introduced Yvette to several of his employees. In total, there were just

27

twelve people who worked for Armstrong Engineering and Computing besides Nicholas, Tom, and Liz. Each was accompanied by a spouse or a friend. Only the young intern, Grant Ziegler, was alone. When Nick introduced Grant to Yvette he was amused to see the effect that Yvette's svelte appearance had on the twenty-four-year-old. Yvette preened beneath the adoration that glowed in the young man's sensitive face.

"Grant, why don't you help Yvette choose what she would like to eat? I have to go and find Tom or Liz and make sure that the company has arranged payment for the Christmas party."

"Sure thing, Nick. Miss Landress, would you care to start with the curries?"

Nick smiled again at the eagerness in the young man's voice. He had accepted Nick's offer with alacrity. Yvette for her part exhibited no show of reluctance. Any personable young male who afforded her the attention she felt her due was an acceptable dinner companion.

Nick grimaced in self-mockery. He did not try to fool himself about his current girlfriend. Their arrangement was strictly ordered to benefit them both. As long as Nick supplied her with small but expensive presents and took her to places where she could show off her figure, she was content to remain with him. And for his part, Nick found her a willing and witty partner who made no demands for a more committed relationship. Yvette, like Nick, wanted no emotional entanglements.

Nick looked around, trying to spot Tom or Liz in the crowded restaurant. Just when he had given up and started to turn toward the buffet he caught a glimpse of blond curls and sapphire cloth.

"Hi, Nick. Wait up." Liz hurried toward him breathlessly. "Tom is parking the car. The baby-sitter was a

28

couple of minutes late and Sammy decided to object to my leaving. Three-year-olds can be a real pain!"

A white grin slashed Nick's handsome features. "And you wouldn't miss a minute of it for all the tea in China. Or should I say India?"

"When in the Khyber you'd better say India," she agreed smoothly as Tom joined them.

Tom's quick look around was filled with comical dismay. "I was afraid something like this would happen when you agreed to let Liz pick the restaurant."

Ignoring her husband, Liz turned to Nick. "What do you think of it?"

"I've eaten Indian food before and liked it, so I'm not overly concerned about my stomach," he teased his friend and manager before continuing seriously. "The atmosphere is very nice. Quiet, subdued, and companionable."

"But?" Liz, too, became serious.

"Oh, it's just me. I can't seem to shake this feeling of depression. I've been here before and really enjoyed being able to see into the kitchen and watch the food being selected and prepared, but today all I see is glass and chrome. It just appears more stark and sterile than I remember from my previous visit."

"Get some of the food," Tom suggested. "That will warm you up, and then some."

Nick laughed and headed toward the buffet, ushering his friends before him.

The curries were highly spiced and very flavorful. The multitude of piquant side dishes had surprised most of the diners in the small party. A few plates, like the sliced tomatoes dressed with a specially seasoned oil, were reassuringly bland and blended well with the crisp chapattis and the puffy puris that added texture to the colorful meal.

"I still can't believe it," Liz moaned, hastily swallowing

29

the contents of her glass of lassi. "Why didn't you warn me?"

Yvette smiled sympathetically. "It's something you have to learn for yourself. I remember the first time Nick brought me here. He did warn me, but I thought he was kidding."

"How can anything so pretty be so dangerous?" Liz continued to wail.

"I know," Yvette agreed. "It's that pretty, cool, green color. No one would ever believe that there must be about a ton of tabasco sauce in it. You have my sympathies, believe me, you really do." Yvette shuddered delicately, remembering her own experience with the fiery, highly seasoned green substance.

"Nick," Liz persisted, "why didn't you warn me?"

"Hmm?" Nick focused vaguely on his office manager. "What did you say?"

"Men!" Liz and Yvette met each other's eyes in mutual understanding. Really, Liz thought to herself, Yvette was much nicer than she had anticipated. Liz turned her gaze back to Nick.

"What were you thinking about anyway?"

A smile pulled at his lips. "Turkeys—and that I miss home cooking, a fireplace . . ." his voice trailed off.

"Really, Nick. You need a wife and a home and children."

Yvette interrupted Liz's catalogue. "I think I'll chat with that nice young man you introduced me to earlier, Nicholas. But before I do," she added benignly, "I think I should tell you that I agree with Liz. You really should get married. And I think that I'll start looking for a new boyfriend."

Yvette leaned over to touch his cheek lightly, then wandered slowly toward the other end of the table where Grant Ziegler became the object of her flattering attention.

Liz frowned worriedly. "Did I put my foot in it?"

"No, not at all. Yvette and I knew where we stood from the start. She is really quite warm and generous beneath that—and I quote—long-legged model figure. But can you imagine Yvette in a kitchen? I doubt she would want to have to renew her acquaintance with spatulas, graters, and kitchen spoons. Tall, svelte redheads prefer to dine out."

Reassured by his imperturbable front, Liz turned the attack closer to home. "That is half your trouble. You are well off. You dress well." Her hand flicked at the sleeve of his perfectly tailored three-piece suit. "And to make matters worse, you are as handsome as all get-out."

Nick grinned amicably. "That doesn't sound like a bad combination."

"But don't you see?" Liz was perfectly serious and more than a little exasperated by his apparent obtuseness. "You draw the non-homey type. They are gorgeous, but most of them think only of their looks and their positions and what you can offer them. They don't have any staying power. But you, typical male that you are, don't see that. Instead, all you see are the externals."

"What's wrong with that?" he asked, amused.

"Everything!" Liz's voice rose. She drew in a long, calming breath. "You have taken to assessing everything in skirts by their standards. But all you are really seeing is the packaging. A small waist, curvaceous hips—and you're interested. You don't even see the homey types, but that's what you need."

A little more disturbed by her assessment than he cared to admit, Nick covered his feelings by baiting her mockingly. "Got anyone particular in mind?"

"Yes!" came the heated reply.

Nick was surprised. "Who?"

"I don't know. I have never seen her, but she will be the complete opposite of Yvette and all the other women you have ever dated. She will be small, petite, and pretty, but not beautiful. She won't care too much if you mess her hair up or kiss all her lipstick off."

"Why petite? I happen to like looking into my date's face without getting a crick in my neck."

"Because you need to feel protective. And she will have to have a mind of her own too."

Clearly puzzled and slightly intrigued by Liz's description of his ideal woman, Nick encouraged her to continue. "I don't follow. Elucidate, my dear. Elucidate and clarify. Your logic escapes me."

Liz laughed at his imitation of their college logic professor. Then she sighed. Men could be so dense sometimes. "It is really quite simple. Didn't you ever take Marriage and the Family?"

"No, I was never heavy into sociology. Suppose you give me a crash course now," he teased.

"Simple. It is a male desire to play the macho he-man. If she is petite, you will be able to feel all macho and protective. You can both enjoy that.

"But she will need a mind of her own to catch and hold your interest. She can't have cotton between her ears. You don't need a paper doll. And you certainly don't need a child's mind in a woman's body. It would never work if you had to protect her from every little thing that happens in life. You are a strong man and you need a strong woman."

"What are the two of you so serious about?" Tom interrupted.

"Getting Nicholas married off." His wife replied seriously.

"Oh, no!" Tom struck a pose that typified melodramatic tragedy. One hand smote his brow while he staggered a few mincing steps and gripped the back of a chair.

"You've finally decided to ask me for a divorce. I knew

it wouldn't last." He bewailed piteously, knowing perfectly well that his beloved wife was still as much in love with him as he was with her.

"I ought to," Liz declared wrathfully. "I'm serious." She referred to the possibility of Nick's entering into the state of holy matrimony.

"But, Liz, honey," Tom now, too, became serious, "why would you want Nick to marry one of those sophisticated types? You're always putting them down."

"Thomas Samuel Jenkins, don't be more stupid than you can help! I don't want him to marry a city girl."

Tom did some rapid review of Nick's usual girlfriends and he couldn't remember Nick having dated any other type since they graduated from high school. "Well, who then?"

"A country mouse," Nick stated dryly.

CHAPTER THREE

Nick arrived home earlier than he had expected. It was barely ten o'clock. As he inserted his key into the security lock of his apartment, Nick reflected that there seemed to be a conspiracy to get him married. When he had taken Yvette home she had suggested that they break off their relationship, insisting that, Nick reflected wryly, domesticity was not her scene. Not at all.

"Liz is right," she had said. "You need a wife. And you are too nice to leave running around loose. Why don't you ask her to fix you up with one of her friends or something?"

Nick had accepted then and there that his relationship with Yvette was at an end. There was no real sorrow that it was ending for either of them, but he was sorry that he would be losing Yvette's companionship as well. She was an interesting and dynamic individual. A very special lady in all respects. He wished her well.

Letting himself into his apartment, Nicholas moved across the foyer and living room without turning on the lights. He reached the bedroom and flipped on the switch.

He blinked in the intense brightness. The room that was revealed by the solitary ceiling light added to his general dissatisfaction. Like his office and like the restaurant, it had been designed to please the eye of the beholder.

Nick grimaced. It must be a phase he was going through. The white walls seemed almost as gray and dirty as the snow he had watched falling earlier in the day. He began to wonder if the pristine fields of white had ever really existed outside his mind. Perhaps they had been a fantasy, a romantic image from a more carefree time. Again he grimaced.

Ignoring the massive bed and dressing table, Nick strode over to the walk-in closet. Rummaging through some of the luggage on the high shelves, he selected two small suitcases. Carrying them with him, he moved back to the bed.

"Looks like this will do it," he murmured to himself, trying to dispel some of his gloomy introspection as he crossed to the bulky dresser. It had been designed in the Spanish tradition, with heavy, dark wood, and tonight it seemed to loom oppressively. Sighing, Nick began removing underclothing and socks from its large drawers.

"I think I'll take only one suit for church; other than that I'll live in blue jeans. I have to admit, I have had enough of the city and city ways for a while."

Nick laughed out loud. "Now I'm talking to myself. Oh, well, they say you only have to worry if you start answering back." Still chuckling, he made a deep mocking bow to his own black-haired reflection in the mirror. Studying himself critically, Nick decided that the charcoal suit was just one more dreary thing about his current life-style. He ran a long-fingered hand through his jet black hair. *Well,* he mused, *I can change that image right now.*

Nick returned to the closet and pulled out a pair of well-worn jeans and a bright red woolen shirt. Returning to stand next to the dramatic brown and orange spread that covered the large bed, he began to shed his suit. He had just pulled on the jeans and tucked the shirt in when a pounding began on his apartment door.

"Now, who in the world—?" He headed through the hall to the foyer. So much for security locked buildings, he reflected dryly. The peephole in the apartment's outer door revealed two men standing before his door. One wore the uniform of the Chicago police department. The other wore a suit that could have been the twin of the one Nick had just removed.

Nicholas released the lock and opened the door. "Yes, can I help you?"

The suited man spoke first. "Are you Nicholas Armstrong?"

"Yes." Nick's voice was businesslike. He stood across the entrance of the door, wanting to make sure of their business before he invited them in. The suited figure extended his hand offering Nick an open wallet displaying his credentials.

"I am Detective Morrison. Could Officer Hastings and I come in and speak with you for a moment?"

Nick examined the credentials, which appeared to be in order. He frowned, unable to think why the police would be calling on him at this time of night.

"Sure." Nick remained brisk and businesslike as he led them into the large living room. The room, now bright with a ceiling light, showed dark-blue carpeting, which acted as a perfect foil for the paler blue of the overstuffed couch and matching armchairs. In the far corner a built-in bar dominated the north wall.

"Have a seat, gentlemen."

"Do you have a drink?" The younger policeman finally spoke.

Nick frowned. In his past experience with the police,

though most of it came from watching television and as an occasional traffic fine during his youth, they had never asked for a drink. "Sure," he shrugged, sounding doubtful. "Help yourself."

The older man frowned briefly. "You misunderstood Officer Hastings. We don't drink on duty. The drink is for you. We wanted to speak with you about your family. There has been a rather serious accident involving your stepmother, and since your father has been unable to reach either you or your friends tonight, he asked us to get ahold of you. I gather that you've been out most of the evening?"

Nick nodded in answer to the older man's last question and accepted the Scotch and soda that the younger man handed him without really noticing it. "How badly was Jill hurt?"

"She's in serious but stable condition, Mr. Armstrong. Your father was anxious to let you know. He knew that you had been planning on returning home tomorrow, but he was hoping that you might be persuaded to catch an earlier flight."

Nicholas frowned. His head was feeling decidedly light and woolly. It must be the shock of hearing that Jill had been hurt. "Sure," he mumbled, his words coming through a tongue that felt unnaturally thick. "I can leave on the first flight in the morning." Nick shook his head, then groaned, wishing he hadn't. "I should tell someone . . ."

"Perhaps your housekeeper," the older man suggested.

A pad and pencil appeared as if by magic in front of Nick's face. He took the writing tools from the younger man. "Yeah, I guess I should leave a note for Mrs. Kerby."

His tongue felt thick and swollen. His head was beginning to spin. He felt himself responding to the voice that began to tell him what to write, but he felt unable to respond to his own mind's commands. The pencil in his hand felt large and awkward. He had to press down to make it leave a trail of words across the white sheet of paper.

"Damn," he spoke shakily. "I feel sick."

The detective's voice was reassuring. "It's just the shock. You'll be fine in a couple of minutes. Here, let Officer Hastings help you." He motioned the uniformed man to assist Nicholas into the bedroom.

When the officer returned, Detective Morrison raised one eyebrow in inquiry.

"Out like a light. That went as smooth as silk."

Detective Morrison looked thoughtful. "Let's hope the rest of it goes as well."

Officer Hastings's short, stubby fingers reached for the Touch-Tone telephone. Tucking the receiver under one ear, he punched a series of numbers and waited for a voice at the other end of the line. "Fatima, tell Zaid we have the *ra'is sa'iman* now."

He hung up the phone and sat down to wait.

Robin was on the last leg of her homeward journey. The early morning sun was just beginning to rise over the glorious Colorado Rocky Mountains, its golden rays turning the blue spruces green and glowing.

Robin sang happily along with the car radio, while her mind reviewed the events of the past few days. She had been to a handicrafts competition in Omaha where some of the entrants had produced some remarkably original work. The winner of the needlepoint contest she had judged was the best of all. "Maybe," she murmured to herself, "I should drop her a line and suggest that she contact some of the eastern design houses."

An hour later she rounded a bend in the road, then

38

slowed her Jeep Wagoneer, downshifted, and pulled into Rifle. She drove slowly through the town, stopping only to do some last-minute grocery shopping and to pick up the mail from the post office box. On her way out of town she stopped in front of a large, blue, two-story house.

She knocked lightly on the door and walked on in. "Hi! June! Are you home?"

"In the kitchen, Robin. Come on in."

Crossing behind the free-standing fireplace, Robin headed toward the kitchen at the far end of the house. "I came bearing gifts."

"*Timeo danos,* or something like that." A carrot-haired freckle-faced woman of indeterminate age grinned cheekily at Robin.

Laughter sparkled in Robin's eyes, turning them into twin lights of jade. "Don't look a gift horse in the mouth, June."

June Marsden reached for the coffeepot that was warming on the stove. "How about a cup?"

"Sure thing, but I really can't stay too long. I want to get home before dark."

June filled a cup and pushed it across the Formica tabletop. "Mmm. I wanted to talk to you about that. Your parents called here—"

"Was anything wrong?" Worry creased her dark brown brows.

"No. Nothing like that," her friend reassured her. "They just forgot that you had that show to go to in Omaha, so they called here wondering if you had decided to spend Christmas with us."

"Oh, good. Everything is going so well, I would hate for Mom to have to face anymore disappointments."

June leaned back in her chair. The two women had been friends ever since June had taken a quilting course that Robin had offered through a local church group two years

39

ago. "No, your parents sounded really happy. I gather that the progress your mother is making is even better than the doctor had first expected."

When Robin nodded enthusiastically, June continued. "I can't tell you how pleased I am for all of you."

"I know." Robin's voice was husky with emotion. "I still can't believe it. Mom will come home walking."

Both women sat in silence, each strongly affected by the wonder of it. June shook off the mood first. She stood up, tying her floral apron tightly around her still-trim figure. "I'm glad you stopped by, I wanted to ask if you'd like to spend Christmas with us, since your folks won't be back in time."

Still lost in pleasant contemplation of her mother's triumphant return, it took a few seconds for June's question to percolate through to Robin's consciousness. "Hmm? Oh, no. No, thanks, June. I want to be home for Christmas. I heard the weather report on the radio this morning. It's supposed to start snowing late tonight and I don't want to be stuck away from home when it starts. You know how the valley is. It would be the middle of January before I'd be able to get back up—especially if it turns out to be a real blizzard."

June frowned. "Frankly, Robin, I don't like the idea of you being there alone."

"Why on earth not?" Robin was astonished.

"What if something happened?" her friend questioned.

"Don't worry about it. Nothing is likely to happen there that couldn't happen anywhere else. Besides, I have a phone and the rangers check in on me every now and then."

Robin continued trying to reassure her friend. "Even if it snows something awful, like it did last year, I can always get out. Dad bought us a couple of snowmobiles and I've got plenty of supplies.

"Besides," she continued to insist when she realized her friend was wavering. "I decided to do Christmas up right. I just bought this huge turkey and all the trimmings. And now I'm on my way to pick up a Christmas tree from Mark Henshaw.

"And believe it or not," Robin pressed home her point, "I really am looking forward to Christmas in the Rockies all by myself. I even unearthed my old Christmas stocking. I'm going to hang it from the mantel."

John Marsden's entry into the kitchen was accompanied by the deep, booming sound of his voice. "What on earth have you been up to, Robin? Your Wagoneer looks like you're going to start a fabric shop up there in your valley."

"No. I was just running low on my supply of sewing goods. I came back from judging a show in Omaha, so I ended up stopping in Denver. I spent the night in a motel and then spent the rest of the morning replenishing my stock."

"Are you staying for Christmas?" John asked.

"No, I want to spend Christmas at home."

"Alone?" He frowned. "There's no need for that, you know. You're welcome here."

"I know, but—"

June interrupted. "Don't press her, John. I already tried. Besides, I want to find out about the show Robin judged in Omaha before she goes."

"If this is going to turn technical, I'll leave." John warned.

"Help yourself to a cookie on your way out," his wife encouraged sweetly.

Still chuckling, he did just that.

The two women spent about another hour discussing the various aspects of quilts and quilting that interested them, and when June finished showing Robin her latest

41

quilt she again asked the younger woman to stay for Christmas.

"No, I'd better not. I really do want to spend Christmas at home. And speaking of home, I'd better leave now or I won't get there until dark."

"Well, if you insist." June still sounded reluctant.

"I'll be fine, June. I'm a big girl now."

"I know, Robin. It's just that I have this mother-hen complex."

"I noticed," Robin inserted dryly, then grinned, knowing that June wouldn't take offense—nor was any meant. She just wanted to be by herself, safe and secure in her mountain retreat. Making her good-byes, Robin promised to come down for New Year's Eve unless the roads were still snowed in.

"I won't count on it then." June grimaced. "If the weather reports are to be believed, it will probably start snowing tonight and keep up for the rest of the week. I doubt that you'll be able to get out before the middle of next month. Have you got enough food?"

Robin was too used to her friend's overly protective attitude to take any offense. The more June thought of you, the more she tried to mother you. Robin's wry grin acknowledged that she was a favorite. "I've got plenty of everything, June. Don't worry. If I need to, I can always take the snowmobile and come down here."

"Drive safe," June cautioned. "It's starting to snow already."

"I will. Merry Christmas."

Robin left the warmth of the large house and walked briskly to her Wagoneer. Large flakes were drifting slowly down from a pale sky. On the final leg of her journey home, the large flakes became smaller and more compact. Their pace was increased dramatically and they left a cold sting in the air. By the time Robin arrived home there was another half inch of snow on the ground. The first thing she did was to call June and let her know that she was home safe.

The rest of the evening Robin spent erecting the huge Christmas tree that Mark Henshaw had saved for her. When it was finally up and decorated, Robin made a big production of hanging her one long red Christmas stocking in front of the blazing fireplace after making sure the firescreen was securely in place.

Stepping back, Robin surveyed the homey scene humorously, thinking that Christmas wasn't really Christmas until the stockings were hung . . . and her father's best Irish whiskey was decanted. Moving slowly, enacting a Christmas ritual that had been a part of her family for generations, Robin moved to the wet bar at the right of the fieldstone fireplace. She poured herself a generous portion of the amber liquid and toasted the Christmas season. A small sip was all she managed as she grimaced at the raw, hot bite of the spirits. She never had liked the taste of whiskey. This Christmas Eve would have to make due with a token toast after all. She set the still-full glass down on the dark wooden countertop and switched off the television set. There would be time enough to clean up the remnants of her Christmas toast tomorrow. Checking the fire one last time, Robin turned off all the lights save those on the Christmas tree, and headed for bed.

CHAPTER FOUR

It was dark and cold. Nick couldn't remember when he had ever been this cold. The jacket he was wearing didn't fit him well. It was large and bulky. Unless he kept it pulled tight at all times, the icy wind would reach in underneath its hem and send shivers up and down his spine. His feet were like blocks of ice. He could not understand why he was wearing shoes rather than boots if he was going for a walk in the woods. He must have forgotten to pack them. And he must have left his gloves at home too.

Everything was so mixed up and confused. Even the woods looked wrong. Except for the past few years, he had always lived near Bloomington, Illinois. He knew that there were woods in the area, but these woods felt all wrong tonight. The ground seemed to be steeper. The trees were the wrong kind; pine and fir were everywhere.

Nick could not remember when the snow had started falling. Maybe it had always been falling. He did know that he was lost. Unless he could find someone to ask directions of, he was not going to be able to get back to his father's house.

He had to get back. His father needed him. Jill had been hurt in an accident and his father had asked him to come home early. Nick stumbled forward, continuing down the mountain.

Time was not real. Hours seemed like minutes and minutes seemed like days. He seemed to be walking constantly, but the scenery never changed. It was always the woods. There were too many trees for it to be a wood. It must be a forest. He stumbled on from tree to tree. Bumping into a heavily ladened branch of a tall conifer, he was suddenly drenched in an avalanche of snow. It slid down the neck of his loose parka and melted against his hot skin. It felt icy cold. He shivered. If I don't find shelter soon . . .

Nick's thoughts halted abruptly. He had come to the edge of the world. The forest gave way to an outcropping of bare rock. Inching his way forward cautiously, he looked out over the valley below.

It was calm. Peaceful. At first glance it seemed uninhabited. A small stream wandered leisurely across the floor of the snow-covered valley. At one point it disappeared for a very short distance. He studied the point where it hid from sight. As his eyes began to focus more readily through the falling snow he noticed a thin white line of smoke rising from a reflecting surface. Water could not smoke; there had to be some kind of shelter down there.

From his vantage point on the outcropping his confused mind was barely able to distinguish a trail of sorts that lead from the aerie where he now stood to the open spread of the white valley below. Perhaps he could find shelter in the valley. It was worth a try.

As he drew closer to the strange edifice, Nick felt that he was approaching an ice castle from the fairy tales of his

45

youth. Snow covered the land. More drifted down from the sky. The building appeared to be made of glass and steel, but unlike the buildings at home, this was not cold and unfeeling. It beckoned and welcomed him.

When he first noticed the colored lights he stopped in his tracks. He feared the lights. They brought a pain and agony of their own. Nick stood very still, like an animal hiding from a predator, in whose very stillness lay its protection. Maybe the lights would not reveal him.

After a while, it could have been minutes or hours, Nick did not know or care which, he began to realize that these lights were different. Their colors were softer. They winked and blinked, but they did not rush at him in whirling, screaming agonies of color. Hesitantly he moved forward, only to be stopped a few feet later by a length of window.

It took some time to find the sliding glass doors, and several seconds more for his numbed fingers to slide the door open. When he finally stumbled into the room he still was not sure that this house did not belong to a magic fairy, a witch, or a wizard. It seemed to have no walls. To his left there was a garden. To the right and behind him glass kept the bitter cold at bay. Before him a fire blazed in a large fieldstone hearth. To its left, lights—soft, colorful lights—twinkled an invitation for him to come forward.

Although still uncertain of the lights, the blazing warmth of the fire drew him irresistibly. As the warmth began to permeate his being, he shed the parka. Standing as close to the blaze as possible, he tried to get warm as shivers chased up and down his spine.

It seemed that a long time passed before he became warm enough to notice the glass on the nearby counter. Shaking fingers closed clumsily around the crystal tumbler. He barely noticed the warmth of the glass in his icy

46

fingers as he concentrated on keeping his hand steady enough to lift the drink to his lips. The raw spirits burned at his throat, making him catch his breath sharply as he reposited the glass on the dark countertop.

The liquid continued its warming path as it flowed down his throat and settled in the empty pit of his stomach. The sudden heat that enveloped him from the inside out made him realize just how chilled to the bone he had been. Slightly more lucid, Nick once again looked around the room. His eyes spotted a warm-looking blanket on one end of the long couch. It was too dark to tell exactly what it looked like, but the way it was folded indicated that it was clean and fresh. Nick made a moue of disgust, acknowledging just how filthy and wet his own clothes were. Once he was warm and dry he could try to find out if there was anyone else in the house.

Nick shed his wet clothing quickly, shivering as the warm air of the fire moved against his overheated skin. He stood naked before the fire, trying to warm his flesh. His large hands used a dry portion of his wool shirt, rubbing his legs and arms and chest briskly, trying to stimulate the circulation of his blood. Considerably warmed by the movement of the coarse cloth, he abandoned his position before the fireplace and walked back to the sofa.

The muscles of his body shone bronze in the firelight. His movements were powerful and strong, yet as graceful as the mountain lion's sleek step.

The blanket, when he reached for it, was not the soft warm wool that he had been expecting. It was a cool fabric, perhaps a cotton or muslin, but it soon became heated by his own body's rising temperature. Wrapping himself tightly in the quilt, he laid down on the couch. If he could just rest for a few minutes he would be in better shape to look for help. As he lay cocooned in the protective warmth, his last conscious thought was that the bold, geometric designs sewn into the quilt somehow reminded him of the rocky outcropping where he had first seen the valley and the sanctuary that this valley itself had offered to him.

Robin woke early on Christmas morning, stretching languidly beneath the soft quilts that covered her. She experienced a vague recollection of waking once during the night. She had not been able to place the noise, but had been so tired from having spent so much time on the road that she had bemusedly thought that it must have been snow sliding off the roof.

Robin grinned at the remembered thought. Stretching once more, she sat up and fumbled for her slippers. She covered her pale green nightgown with a matching robe, and wandered down the hall to the kitchen.

After a light breakfast Robin filled the kitchen sink with soapy water and started to wash the few dishes she had used. Remembering the unfinished whiskey from the night before, she headed into the front room. Her step was quick and sure. The lively mass of her long brown hair swung saucily with each step. Reaching for the tumbler was an automatic gesture, but her fingers froze midway.

A dark, puzzled frown marred her brow. "I could have sworn . . ." she mumbled to herself, then shrugged.

Just as her fingers closed around the empty glass she froze once again. Something dark huddled near the hearth. Muscles tensed and stomach churning, she held her position for a full minute before she slowly turned toward the dark shape. More seconds passed as she finally recognized the pile for what it was: torn and ragged clothing!

Oh, God! Someone's in the house! A chill of fear danced along the vertebrae of Robin's spine. Her knees sagged a little. Taking a deep breath, she forced herself to think rationally. If she could get to the garage . . . if she could take the snowmobile . . . No. That was impossible. One look out her bedroom window this morning had been enough to tell her that several more inches of snow had accumulated during the night and it was still falling heavily. The weatherman's six to ten inches was going to be a lot closer to ten to sixteen. She would have to dig the garage out first. No. She would have to think of something else.

Biting her lip in an attempt to remain calm, Robin turned, intending to head back to the kitchen. She would feel better if she had some sort of protection. Her eye caught the long figure of a man who lay wrapped in her newest quilt. A roaring noise rushed into her ears and filled her mind. For a moment she wondered if she was going to faint, but she managed to gain a somewhat tentative hold over her fears. However, it still took a few precious heartbeats to realize that the powerful, frightening, bare-chested figure was asleep.

Courage returned slowly. Robin edged her way into the kitchen. She searched the silverware drawer, looking for a long sharp knife. She was stunned by the events of the morning, yet still maintained enough presence of mind to realize that with the storm raging outside it would take the sheriff hours to arrive. And then it might be too late.

How on earth had the man gotten in? Could she have left a door unlocked? No, she had checked each of the locks . . . or had she? She had been caught up in Yuletide memories last night. Perhaps she hadn't checked all the doors. How could she have been so careless? *Oh, damn!* she berated herself as she found what she was looking for.

Returning to the front room, she stood just out of reach of the long, powerfully muscled arms that held a small corner of the Cathedral Mountain quilt to a wide expanse of chest. He looked uncomfortable on the six-foot-long

49

couch. Robin shivered, deciding that he must be close to six foot three or four.

One long narrow foot stuck out from under the quilt that hid but outlined his powerful legs and thighs. His narrow hips were barely covered decently. A fine layer of jet black hair ran from his navel to his chest, spreading out over the powerful pectoral muscles like a coat of armor. Her artist's eye automatically took in the flat plane of his stomach.

He would make a fantastic model, she thought irrelevantly as she lifted a hand to her nape trying to ease some of her tension.

The long column of his bearded throat looked as strong as the rest of him. His right hand was flung across his eyes. The fingers were long and tapered. His fingernails were evenly cut and well manicured, although the hand itself was badly bruised and scraped.

What bothered Robin the most was her own reaction to the virile-looking man who lay naked beneath her quilt. She should have been terrified out of her wits, but instead she felt stunned and afraid, but stunned disbelief was predominant.

The man appeared to be in his early thirties, although it was hard to tell with the beard. His scruffy face looked vulnerable in repose. Glancing at the full, sensual lower lip, Robin felt an unfamiliar tingling in the pit of her stomach. *I must be getting cabin fever.*

Looking at him more closely, she noticed that his blue-black hair was matted and caked. The broad forehead showed a slight purple discoloration of a bruise and his high cheekbones were flushed as though with fever. His firm lips parted over even white teeth as his body labored to drag air in and out of his lungs.

Robin inched forward cautiously, her eyes wary. If he moved, she wouldn't hesitate in protecting herself. She

50

transferred the knife to her left hand and touched his face with the back of her free hand. His cheek above the growth of beard burned like fire. She moved her hand to rest palm-down over the center of his chest. His heartbeat was reassuringly steady, but his feverish skin beneath the tips of her fingers was moist. Her fingers tensed slightly at the springy feel of the dark cloud of hair that covered his chest.

He looked too ill to hurt her, she thought as she laid the knife absently on the coffee table. Reaching for the boldly patterned quilt that he had pushed down around his hips, Robin pulled it up over his shoulders, tucking it firmly around him.

Stepping back away from his sleeping form, she made a wry face. "Just what I've always wanted to find under my tree on Christmas morning," she murmured with irony.

Moving back to the fireplace, she stooped to pick up the man's discarded clothes. They were still wet to the touch and filthy. Turning thoughtfully, she wondered what kind of accident he had been in or if he was lost. He didn't look like the type to go speeding around blind curves in the middle of a Colorado snowstorm; and her home was definitely off the beaten track—even summer tourists didn't usually drop by.

She went through each of the pockets of the clothing looking for some sort of identification or some clue as to who the man was. She found nothing—nothing but a few bloodstains on the torn parka. Still unnerved, she gave a heartfelt sigh of exasperation before draping the soggy clothing over a nearby chair to dry.

"Damn!" she muttered to herself. "So what do I do now?" Arms crossed protectively around herself, Robin tried to think, not realizing just how vulnerable she looked, while she seriously contemplated phoning the sheriff. However, she soon decided against making the call. Looking out the floor-to-ceiling windows of the house only confirmed what her ears had already told her. The storm was even now increasing in intensity. She could not see the stand of pine only a couple of hundred yards from the house. Even if she were able to get the call through, the sheriff wouldn't be able to send anyone up until the storm abated somewhat, and since her unwelcome visitor had no identification, the sheriff wouldn't be able to tell her anything about him or even notify the man's family.

Feeling ill at ease in her robe, Robin changed into a white sweater and jeans. As the morning wore on, some of her tension subsided. She was still nervous and fearful, but the man lay so still and silent that eventually her mind turned more and more toward his condition. She couldn't even begin to guess how he had come to be hurt and ended up on her couch. As she glanced at the dark bruise on his forehead she wondered if he had a concussion. She hoped not, for she had little training in first aid, and the experiences of helping her mother with her exercises and in and out of her wheelchair weren't going to be a lot of use if something was seriously wrong with her uninvited guest.

When the mantel clock struck noon Robin went into the kitchen to fix herself a cup of tea. Her queasy stomach wouldn't allow anything heavier. When she was finished she walked quietly back into the front room, intending to check once more on the man.

She was more than halfway into the room before she realized that he was no longer asleep. Broad muscular shoulders rested against the back of the roughly textured brown couch. His bare legs and equally bare thighs were stretched out in front of him. The Cathedral Mountain quilt's bold geometric design played up his superb masculinity. He presented an extremely virile appearance, especially with the quilt hunched carelessly around his lean

52

hips. Yet it was not his overwhelming masculinity that held her motionless. It was the knife.

The long sharp blade glinted in the early afternoon light. His dark cobalt-blue eyes stared at its wickedly sharp edge, as his hand turned it slowly. Inspecting it. Testing it.

Robin's brain was screaming. *The knife! I forgot the knife! I left it lying on the table!* Panic rose within her. She tried to assess the situation quickly and rationally. She doubted if she would be able to make it back into the kitchen before he could catch her. His muscled legs looked capable of running her down easily, and he undoubtedly topped her by a good ten inches and by at least seventy pounds. Even ill he would be able to capture her and hold her effortlessly. Besides, if she did make it, he still had the sharp knife.

Robin saw no avenue of escape. If this giant of a man meant to harm her, she stood no chance. He handled that knife as if he was assessing its value as a weapon. To fight would mean certain death. A sob tore at her throat.

The man's heavy-lidded gaze turned toward her, impaling her. His cobalt eyes automatically assessed her petite figure, examining the fullness of her breasts, the smallness of her waist, the curving contours of her hips. It was a stripping look.

Her hand fluttered to her breast, pressing against her pounding heart, trying to still its thunderous beat. The movement drew his eyes upward again, allowing him to make a more thorough assessment of her features.

He gripped the knife and sat stiffly upright on the sofa. "Who the hell are you?" he snarled.

The total unexpectedness of it shocked Robin. If he had come at her—or demanded that she come to him—she would have been prepared. But no. This great, huge beast snarled and snapped as though she had no right to be in her own home.

Fury replaced her fear, her anger igniting twin flames of icy green fire in her eyes. "That's a fine thing to say—I live here. Who the hell are *you*? Which is more to the point. You are my unwelcome guest!" Robin seethed furiously.

"I am terribly sorry." His apology was politely urbane, suggesting a too-early guest apologizing to a running-behind-schedule hostess. "Did I arrive at an inconvenient time?"

Robin's mouth fell open.

"I will go if you like," the man stated, apparently willing to please.

Still Robin made no move, uttered no sound.

Nick raised one hand, placing it on the quilt that precariously covered his hips.

"No!" Robin was galvanized at last by his impending total nudity.

"Shall I stay?"

"No," she repeated less forcefully.

"Well, I'll leave then." Nick sighed. Sometimes one's hostess could be so difficult to please.

"But—but you don't have any clothes on." Robin felt as if she were babbling.

"Oh." Nick paused. His blue eyes clouded with confusion. This was certainly a strange party.

"Where are my clothes?" His voice held only mild curiosity.

"Over there." Robin's voice was a mere thread as she pointed to the hearth. She must be going mad. This insane conversation could not be real. She would wake up soon. This was just a nightmare brought on by June's concern and too much work and worry. She would wake up and

54

the whiskey would still be there and the man would be gone.

"Well, I'll go get them then." His low voice was softly soothing. He spoke as though talking to a fractious child.

"No!" his hostess almost screamed.

"Whyever not?" he answered her mildly.

"You've got my quilt—" She lifted a shaking hand to her brow.

"Do you want it first?" Again his hand moved as if to lift a corner.

"No!" Her voice was shrill. "You great, hulking brute. You can't go parading around my house naked as a jay-bird!" Her nerves had stretched to the breaking point and beyond.

"Why not?" Her vocabulary seemed quite limited, but when her eyes snapped and her hair whirled around her sexy figure, he could almost forget her odd behavior.

"Now how in hell do I answer that?" Robin mumbled to herself, wondering why she hadn't accepted June's hospitality after all. The man was obviously an escapee from the local asylum.

"I am sorry, but I didn't hear you." His voice remained polite.

Robin looked at the man sharply. She was beginning to suspect that he was trying to tease her. His expression was pleasantly befuddled. Nothing else.

"Because I don't want to see you naked," she snapped, unsure of what else she could say.

"Oh." He thought about that for a while. "Why don't you just close your eyes?" he suggested.

Robin did just that in exasperation and fury. She raged inwardly. *Give me strength!*

"I don't want to close my eyes." Then she blushed furiously at what she had actually said. Heaven only knew what her tormentor would make of that.

Nick sighed. His head was starting to throb abominably. He felt cold and she wasn't making any sense at all.

"I could close mine," he offered hopefully.

Robin didn't utter a sound. His answer stunned her. His logic eluded her. How could his closing his eyes prevent her from seeing him.

"My head hurts." The man interrupted her thoughts with a plaintive note in his attractive baritone. "Could I lie back down?"

"Please." Robin's voice wobbled dangerously. Torn between laughter and tears, in a mild state of stunned, disbelieving shock, she watched the tall man lie back down on the couch. He pulled the quilt snugly around him, hunching it up over his shoulders as well as drawing it down around his feet. His long jet lashes fluttered once, twice, and then no more.

Robin put her hands to her face, breathing out a long, shaky sigh. She could feel her limbs begin to tremble as reaction set in. Hastily, and with a clumsiness born of unease, she lowered herself into a chair, trying to draw deep, slow, steadying breaths. At last her heartbeat slowed and her breathing became more normal. Her fingers began to relax their stranglehold from the arms of her chair. She laid her head back to rest against the cushions. Her cinnamon-colored hair contrasted brightly with the dark brown of the chair. She drew another steadying breath. No one, but no one, would ever believe this.

She got up slowly to walk over to where her uninvited guest now lay sleeping peacefully. It took a fair amount of effort to keep her hand from trembling as she picked up the murderous-looking knife and headed back to the kitchen.

The knife had not been much help, not to her.

CHAPTER FIVE

The four people who sat in the old-fashioned kitchen of
the Armstrong farmhouse near Bloomington shared a
common bond and had experienced a series of shared
emotions. Stunned disbelief, shock, outrage, and fear.
Fear was the strongest.

"I still can't believe it." Liz's voice was shaky. She had
been crying again.

Her husband ran one tired hand through his sandy hair
before patting his wife's shoulder.

"Are you sure you and Jill want us here, Max?" Tom's
voice was tired.

"Yes." The older man's face was drawn.

Jill's long fingers squeezed her husband's arm. Touching him offered her some comfort. She noticed absently
that in times of stress couples tended to touch more. It
seemed that it was an unspoken bond of communication
that afforded both the giver and the recipient a measure
of comfort.

"We were glad you came. But I feel sorry that you

didn't bring the kids. It would have been fine. They might have cheered us up," said Jill.

"And kept our minds off Nick," Max added.

Liz shook her head. "No, they would have just kept pestering us to tell them where Nick was." Liz smiled with affection. "He spoils them something awful, especially Candy."

Jill suggested hesitantly, "Would you mind telling us again what you found."

Tom shrugged. "I don't know any more now than when I spoke with you on the telephone last week."

Liz was more willing. "Why not, Tom? Maybe if we start at the beginning, we can pool all of what we know. I still don't have all of it straight in my own mind."

"Besides," Jill inserted, "telephones are so impersonal. I don't think we took it all in."

Tom shrugged again. Talking wasn't going to help, but he offered no further resistance.

Silence filled the farm kitchen. The small yellow parakeet in the corner gave an inquiring chirp, startling the four human occupants.

"Okay," Liz started. "Last time we saw Nick was at the Christmas party. We had all been out to eat at Khyber's. I talked to Yvette a couple of days later, and—"

Jill interrupted, "Yvette Landress?"

"Mmm. She was Nick's girlfriend," Liz agreed.

"Was?" Maxwell Armstrong's voice was harsh. The use of the past tense in reference to his only son sent another shaft of fear spiraling down his spine.

"When Liz talked to Yvette she said that she and Nick had decided to break off their relationship after they left us on Friday night," Tom inserted hastily.

"Anyway," Liz continued, "Yvette said Nick left her place around nine o'clock."

"We knew that he intended to catch a commuter flight

58

the next day, so when you called it really came as a shock."

Max nodded. "When Nick didn't come in on Saturday's flight, I wasn't really worried. We had talked about the possibility earlier, and I knew that he wanted to finish up one of his accounts, so I figured that he would be coming in the next day. But when he still didn't show up on Sunday, and when I couldn't get him at home or at work . . . well, I had Jill try you at work."

Tom pushed his cup of cold coffee away. "I went right over, Max. You know that. I called you and told you so earlier. When I got there I had to have the manager let me in. The apartment was fine; nothing appeared to have been moved. Even the police said that there didn't appear to be a struggle. Apparently Nick must not have suspected anything."

Tom stood and walked to the window, looking out across the snow-covered fields. His eyes moved absently. Their beauty did not register on his consciousness. Instead, the scene appeared bleak, stark, lifeless—a barren waste.

"His suitcase was partially packed. Perhaps he was interrupted. I don't know. I started going through the papers on his desk to see if I could find out where he was when I first noticed the notes. The one, Mrs. Kerby's, was in Nick's handwriting, although toward the end of it, it was practically illegible. It said something about Jill having an accident and you wanting him to come home."

"What about the other one?" Jill asked.

Tom did not answer for a few moments. "It was one of those with pasted-up letters. All it said was, 'If you want Armstrong, drop the Arab contracts. You have until Christmas.' "

Liz began to explain. "Nick took on that contract about six months ago. Now the country is filled with political

59

unrest. Apparently one of the terrorist groups found out that we were working on designing some sophisticated machinery for the current government."

Max frowned. "I thought Nick refused to accept their work."

"Not all of it, only part," Tom supplied. "We turned down the work they wanted for their military, but we accepted the contract for the oil industry."

No one said anything for a few minutes. Jill stood up and poured herself another cup of coffee. "Anyone else?"

Liz and Tom refused, but Max accepted a cup. "What happened next?"

"I called the police first. The rest you know. They called in the FBI and they called in the—the list is endless. And the upshot of all this is that nothing"—his voice was bitter—"*nothing* is being accomplished."

"Now, Tom." Liz tried to be fair. "You know there isn't a lot any of us can do. The officials did make inquiries."

"Sure, they questioned all our employees, all Nick's friends, and all his neighbors. But I don't see anyone under arrest and I don't see Nick back here where he belongs."

"They are doing all that they can. They did find out how Nick was taken away without arousing anyone's suspicions." Liz turned to the Armstrongs. "They were really clever. No one would question an ambulance and policemen."

Max's voice echoed the bitterness in Tom's. "So, where does that leave us now?"

"Nowhere."

Liz tried again. "The FBI agent indicated that they would have some news for us before too long. This can't go on. They'll find him soon. They have to." A tear ran down her face.

Jill stood up briskly. "What we need is some lunch."

Her husband snapped with irritation. "How can you think of food now?"

"We have to eat, Max. Besides, it gives me something to do."

Max apologized, knowing that he was short-tempered because of worry and that he was overreacting.

Liz helped Jill fix lunch while the two men took the collies for a short walk. When they all sat down at the table no one did more than pick at their food. Jill was scraping the last of the untouched plates down the disposal when a knock sounded at the back door.

Two clean-shaven men in three-piece suits entered. Before either could say a word Max pulled them forward. "Have you any news? Is my son—" His voice broke.

The youngest man's voice was compassionate. "We have had some information about the people who took your son, but unfortunately not a lot about Mr. Armstrong."

He continued. "We know the group that was behind the kidnapping and we have made a number of arrests. The group that was active in Chicago made all the arrangements to pick up your son. When we started getting close they also made arrangements to fly your son to another area."

"Do you know where?" Jill pleaded softly.

"Yes, Mrs. Armstrong. They planned to fly by private plane to the L.A. area."

Liz's voice was excited. "Then you will be able to get Nick when they land in Los Angeles?"

The agents' expressions clouded. The older one sighed. This was never easy. "No, ma'am, not exactly."

"What—what do you mean?"

"Mrs. Jenkins, isn't it?" When she nodded he continued. "We arrested several of the members in the Chicago area. They reported that Mr. Armstrong had been

61

moved. They knew we were closing in. Mr. Armstrong was valuable to them, so they decided to move him before we could close in. We know that they took a six-seater plane. They refueled at a small private landing strip outside of Sterling, Colorado. From there they were to fly to another private landing strip just west of Cedar City, Utah. They were to arrive in Cedar City late last night."

Tom's voice was defeated. "You said *were*?"

The agent tried to maintain his objectivity. "The plane did not land on schedule. We know that the weather was bad over the Rockies. We expect that they took shelter somewhere until the storms end."

Max entered the conversation. "Tell me truthfully, what are Nick's chances?"

There was a pause. The agent knew from his reports that Maxwell Armstrong suffered from a heart condition. As he opened his mouth, intending to present a slightly more optimistic view, Max interrupted.

"Does Nick have any chance?"

"I won't lie to you, Mr. Armstrong. If they made shelter, he has some chance. If they went down in the storm, I would say almost none. And—" Again the agent hesitated. They would need to know sooner or later.

Max's voice was grief-stricken. "And even if they get to shelter, we can't expect that they will keep Nick alive. He is expendable. They would have to kill him eventually. When they didn't let him go after Tom started running those announcements on the radio and television and newspapers that the company would drop the Arab contracts, I knew. I guess I knew it all along."

Jill moved behind her husband, placing her arms around his waist. "Don't, darling, we don't know that Nick is dead."

Max's voice was choked. Every person in the room was affected by it. Even the two agents shared in his agony. "I just feel so helpless." His fist banged against the wall. "God, is there nothing we can do?"

Jill's voice was low, a mere whisper. "We can pray, Max. It's all we can do."

Robin placed the knife carefully back in the drawer of the kitchen cupboard. Storm or no storm, she was going to have to call the sheriff's department. This was not something she felt capable of handling any longer. Her hand reached for the kitchen extension.

When it rang underneath her fingers it nearly scared her to death. Fumbling, she dropped it, causing it to crash loudly into the silence that followed.

"Hello?" Robin's voice was shaking.

"Hello, Babe, what's going on?" Her father's hearty voice greeted her tentative question.

"Oh, Daddy."

"Robin, what's the matter?"

Robin got a grip on herself. How could she tell her parents that their house had been invaded and that she had been holding a perfectly inane conversation with an escaped lunatic from the Mad Hatter's tea party?

Robin laughed weakly, thinking how he probably would have offered to get up and carry the tea tray too.

"Nothing's wrong, Daddy. I just miss you and Mom. This is the first Christmas we've been apart in a long time, that's all."

They chatted for some time, but Robin's mind was only half on what she said; the other half of her mind was fully occupied with the dilemma of her unwelcome boarder. She was only partially aware that her mother had picked up an extension phone and joined in on the conversation. Robin's answers must have made sense to the other two people on the line, though, for after a few minutes of conversation they thanked Robin for the gifts she had sent and asked if theirs had arrived in time.

"Yes. They're all here. I put up a Christmas tree and they're under it," she answered absently.

"You mean to say that you haven't opened them yet?" Margaret was astonished. The Robin she knew hated to wait fifteen minutes, let alone half the day.

Robin could have bitten off her tongue in frustration. So much for trying to act natural. Not wanting to upset her parents, especially when they could have done nothing but worry, she hedged. "I got back late from the show I was judging. I got up only a little while ago."

Her father's booming voice teased across the wires. "Well, Babe, were you a good little girl this year? Did you find something special under the tree?"

Robin swallowed hard, for once wishing that she still was "Daddy's little girl," wishing that she could run to him with her problems and have him make everything turn out all right. "I—unh— Yeah, sort of."

Not recognizing his daughter's unusually high tone of voice over the crackling line, Lewis laughed heartily. "I'll bet it was chocolates." He knew his daughter's weakness.

"No." Robin schooled her voice to a lower, firmer tone, wanting to tell them the truth, but not daring.

The line began to crackle ominously.

"Sounds as if the lines might go down at any minute," Lewis warned.

"Yes, the weather out here is something fierce. It started sometime last night. I can't even make out the stand of pine near the house."

"Well, we'd better let you go. I can hardly hear you anymore." Her father was equally hard to hear through the crackling.

"I love you, Daddy," Robin practically shouted. She needed them now, but could not tell them why.

64

"We love you too, Babe."

"Merry Christmas, darling," her mother added.

Robin hung up the receiver after hearing her parents disengage the line at their end. She lifted it again to call the sheriff. Her fingers fumbled with the buttons. She heard the phone at the other end start to ring—then complete silence.

It did not really come as a surprise. She had known that the line was going when she spoke to her parents. But she had not wanted to act unnaturally. It would have upset them, and if they were worried, it would only retard her mother's progress. Robin could not allow that to happen. She hung up the dead receiver and sat down at the kitchen table. Crossing her arms on the table in front of her, she laid her head down on them.

"I am not going to cry." The words were choked.

When Robin finally straightened from the kitchen table it was dark. She could not believe that she had sat there so long. Her mind was a complete blank. She could not even remember what her thoughts had been. She lifted her long hair off the back of her neck and rubbed her nape. She felt cramped from the position she had maintained for so long. Sighing deeply, she supposed that she should check on the man in the front room. There really did not seem to be much else to do. There was no place she could go and no one that she could contact. She would have to deal with whatever happened by herself.

Robin noted that the wind was still gusting although the snow had appeared to stop. The sky was almost black in comparison to the whiteness of the ground. The swirling clouds of snow danced like graceful ballerinas dipping and swaying in time to a frenzy of music. Occasionally a gust of wind would disturb their paths by adding a whirling dervish to the choreography. It was beautiful—and dangerous. Just like the man. Even with several days growth of beard Robin could tell that he was handsome. Whether he proved to be dangerous would be something she would have to wait and see.

He had turned on his stomach. His right arm cradled his head, which was turned toward her. His left arm was clear of the covers and hung down the couch resting against the floor. The muscled shoulders were smooth, the black hairs on his forearm hid its flesh from her view, but the hand looked large and strong.

Robin eyed his length again. His long legs were drawn up under the covering quilt. His cheeks were still flushed with fever, but his breathing seemed to be less labored.

She stared at the sleeping form. "If you were green, I would call you the Incredible Hulk."

One sleepy blue eye opened to survey her lazily.

Robin started in surprise. She had not realized that the man was awake. A shiver of apprehension moved down the length of her spine. How long had he been awake? Had he heard her on the telephone? Could he know that the lines were down? *Stop it, Robin!* she cautioned herself sternly. There was no way he could know. She was just being paranoid.

Taking a stern hold of her flagging courage, Robin drew herself up to her full height—unimpressive though it may have been. Trying to sound in complete control of the bizarre situation, she asked smoothly, "What's your name?"

"Nick." The man paused, then smiled—a small, secret smile that made Robin feel entirely too vulnerable.

His voice sounded lazy, indolent, almost bemused. "Are you the Snow Queen? You don't look like the one in the book." His blue gaze wandered over her face and figure. She didn't look cold like the Snow Queen had; she looked warm and inviting. Her cinnamon-colored hair was warm and rich. Her skin had a golden glow like the summer sun,

Not understanding his reference to a Snow Queen, and feeling decidedly uneasy under his glittering regard, Robin deemed that it would be prudent to ignore his question. "Do you have a last name?"

She was amazed to see a wariness come to his eyes. And she knew that at this particular moment he was perfectly lucid.

Nick stiffened at the intrusive question. He remembered voices saying his name over and over again. Every time he heard it he had also heard contempt and accusation. And there had been discomfort, even pain. He did not want to remember. Forcing his mind to relax, Nick let his eyes roam around the room. Behind her the snow was swirling in the darkness. Her white sweater stood out from the darkness. Its pattern of Christmas holly seemed to be reflected throughout the room. His eyes moved again, noticing the huge Christmas tree. Nick smiled vaguely. Someone had been very generous. Gifts were piled high under the tree.

Fear made Robin's voice sharper than normal. "What's your last name?"

His eyes moved back to impale the woman who was badgering him. "Saunders," he lied. "Nick Saunders."

Forcing herself not to take a step backward was one of the hardest things Robin had ever done. This man was a total unknown. One minute he seemed harmless, even helpless, then suddenly he represented a danger more frightening than anything else she had ever known. Her tongue felt dry as she traced the edge of her upper teeth. "How did you get here?"

Nick frowned, then turned over, preparatory to sitting up.

"No, no. Don't get up," Robin insisted. She damned well wasn't going to play peek-a-boo with that quilt this time.

Nick lay back down obediently. His eyes closed. A long-fingered hand raked through his wavy black hair, snagging in the mats and snarls. He frowned more deeply this time, his brows forming an almost straight line across his forehead. His head hurt abominably. He gave a long, low sigh. "I don't know. Does it matter? I think I walked."

"Were you alone?" She persisted in her queries, hoping to find out more about the intruder, hoping to hear something that would calm her nerves.

He considered the question for some time before answering, making Robin wonder if he was telling the truth. "Yes, I was alone." Suddenly his stomach growled loudly, startling them both.

Robin choked back a nervous cough as he pushed the quilt down around his hips, and placed his hand against his flat stomach. *Maybe I will play peek-a-boo with that damned quilt after all,* she thought.

"Did I—Was that—?" Nick's expression was the epitomy of surprise.

Robin tried for nonchalance. "Are you hungry?"

The man thought it over carefully, giving the question all the consideration due one of earth-shattering importance.

"I'm not sure. I think so."

Robin coughed again. She had to get hold of herself. "Stay there. I'll go make you something."

"I'll come with—"

Here we go again! "No. You stay there."

This time Robin had managed to have the presence of mind to draw his attention to the tattered clothing that hung over a chair near the hearth. "When I have gone, you can get up and put those on. Then you can come out into the kitchen if you want. It's just past the garden. Okay?"

"Okay." He closed his eyes, lying back.

Robin left quickly before he could change his mind.

CHAPTER SIX

Robin banged a saucepan down on the burner of the gas stove, trying to decide whether anger or fear should be her predominant emotion. This whole situation was completely crazy and way out of hand. Nothing would have pleased her more than to have shown her unwelcome visitor out the door, but, instead, she found herself in the dubious position of having offered to fix him a meal.

The man was bizarre. The situation was bizarre. Her own behavior was bizarre! Fuming, Robin glanced balefully at the contents of the kitchen cupboard. She may have been fool enough to offer to feed the man, but she was damned if she was going to go to any trouble doing it. He could eat something out of a can, and if he didn't like it, he could just lump it! Or leave! "Now, there's a thought," she muttered to herself as she opened the can that held the least appeal.

It took a second for the flash of movement she saw out of the corner of her eye to register. She turned quickly to face the open area of the garden and hall. As she backed up against the stove her expression was wary and filled with caution—but not fear.

The man—Nick—padded into the kitchen as though it were his own home. His rangy body leaned against the kitchen sink as if it were an old friend. Robin experienced an unusual feeling of claustrophobia. His blatant masculinity brought a flutter to her stomach. Then amusement took the place of her earlier wariness.

Doesn't he like to wear clothes? The only apparent concession to decency he had made was to pull on the faded blue jeans. And they were not leaving all that much to her imagination. Their torn and bedraggled state gave her a glimpse of his hairy leg, bony knee, and muscular thigh. The shiny buckle of his wide leather belt drew her eye to his massive chest. His shirt dangled limply from one dark hand, and his feet were bare.

Robin motioned him to sit down at the small kitchen table, then turned her attention back to the bubbling stew. She dished it up quickly and placed it on a quilted place mat directly in front of him. He sat watching her intently as she moved to sit across the table from him. Robin could not tell what he was thinking, but his eyes never left hers.

"It's called Ham and Veggies," she offered helpfully.

Slowly his eyes lowered to the bowl in front of him. He stared at it but made no attempt to touch it.

"It tastes better than it looks," she encouraged.

Nick picked up his spoon and took a cautious taste. Gradually the tempo of his spooning in of the stew increased. Soon he had finished the entire bowl. Only then did he look up again, his expression hopeful.

"Is there any more?"

Robin frowned. He had wolfed down the entire bowl as if there were no tomorrow. "Yes," she hesitated. "There's plenty, but don't you think you had better take it a little

70

slowly? I don't think you even stopped to chew that last helping."

A peculiar look crossed his bearded features. A spasm of pain gripped his insides, forcing the words through tight lips. "I think I'm going to be sick."

Robin moved quickly to his side. She could see that the knuckles of one hand shone white as he gripped the edge of the table. It was obvious that he was trying to force down the bile that had risen in his throat. Solicitously, she helped him to the sink.

When the retching stopped she wiped his face and hands with a cool cloth. She could feel the heat that emanated from his body. He was burning up.

"I hope you're not going to be ill. There's no way on earth I can get a doctor up here."

He shook his head mutely, then groaned and swayed dizzily.

Leading him back to the table, Robin helped him to slide back down into the chair again. Once he was propped over the table, she went down the hall to her parents' room. Her movements were swift and economical. She pulled the covers and the top sheet down from the bed then returned to the kitchen for Nick. He was shaking uncontrollably, shivering with fevered chills and the aftershock of his sickness.

He leaned heavily on her, staggering the short distance into the large bedroom. She eased him onto the bed where he lay, arms flung wide, covering an astonishing amount of the mattress. He was even larger and longer and broader than Robin had first realized. The Incredible Hulk was appropriate after all.

Robin eyed him ruefully. Fate, it seemed, had put in her own two cents worth. Apparently she was going to see a lot more of this bearded giant than she had originally planned on.

71

Leaning over his shivering form, Robin loosened the silver buckle of his wide belt. Her fingers hesitated briefly after undoing the snap at the waistband of his jeans before resolutely reaching for the zipper. She tried to ease them down over his lean hips, but he was just too heavy for her to manage alone.

She shook his shoulder briefly. Nick opened his eyes. The glazed pupils tried, and failed, to focus. Robin made her voice brisk. "Lift up your hips. I'll help you take off your jeans."

Nick stared uncomprehendingly. A deep scowl knit his brows. "Wha—?" He mumbled thickly. "Don't feel good. Go 'way."

An unexpected smile flitted round the corners of Robin's mouth. He sounded just like a tired and stubborn six-year-old. She changed her tactics, making her voice sound firm but persuasive. A mother's voice to her child. "Lift your hips, Nick. Be a good boy."

Giving a tired grunt, the man complied.

Robin eased the torn jeans down over his narrow hips. He was asleep before she finished removing them from his long legs. The white cotton briefs that he wore where thrown into stark relief by his darly tanned skin. Smiling wryly, Robin patted his bearded cheek. "I'm beginning to get the hang of conversing with you, Mr. Saunders. A few more times and we might actually move from the pitifully absurd to the almost relevant."

Robin eased the covers up over his sleeping form, tucking them around him securely. His breathing was regular although a trifle shallow. She concluded that he was more likely to be exhausted than to have a concussion.

She returned to the kitchen and cleaned up. When she finished, Robin switched off the lights and moved through the garden area into the dining room and down the three shallow steps that led to the front room. Tonight she checked each door carefully. She had had her fill of unexpected company.

Restless, she switched on the stereo. The soft strains of the easy-listening music of KOSI filtered through the house. She straightened the front room as if by rote, then eyed the Christmas tree, the pile of gifts under it still high. She did not feel like opening them just now. She left the colorful tree lights twinkling in the darkness as she turned off the overhead lights and continued on her circuit.

One final check of the garage door entrance and Robin headed down the hall and into the study. She walked slowly over to the built-in chests and rummaged through them for her latest project. When she found it she sorted through a collection of fine crewel yarn and chose a handful of colorful skeins. She carried the thread and the linen along with her workbasket into the room where the man lay sleeping restlessly.

Sighing, she pulled up an armchair and decided to keep watch over him. The soft music soothed her nerves and she settled back in her chair, letting the music wash over her and relax her as she began to sew.

About eleven o'clock Nick began to thrash about. His delirium increased over the next couple of hours. His words were disjointed and slurred, many of them making little sense to the woman who listened. He spoke of Yvette, and Liz, and Jill who was hurt. He harshly condemned the police and people who called his name and the stabbing pains of his head. He spoke of floating and of pain gripping his mind and whirling agonies of color and light. Of blood and cold and ice castles in the air. Several times he tried to get up and go to his father's house. It took a great deal of Robin's strength of body and mind to dissuade him from leaving the bed.

He was wringing wet with sweat and shivering when the air touched his overheated body. Robin left him for a few minutes to fetch a bowl of warm water and a couple of cloths. She began to sponge his fevered body. When he relaxed a little she cleansed the dried blood from his dark hair, noticing that he had a slight scalp wound in addition to the bruise on his forehead. Apart from his scraped hands, she saw no other visible wounds. The fever continued to burn, although he thrashed about a good deal less. Robin changed the water several times, placing one cloth over his forehead and eyes while she gently wiped the fever-induced perspiration from his torso and limbs.

A little after two o'clock in the morning his fever broke. His restless movements ceased. He lay perfectly still. His breathing was regular and even. He looked comfortable and content.

Robin raked a tired hand through her long brown hair. She felt anything but calm, cool, and collected. Perspiration trickled down her back and her sweater felt sticky, itchy, and prickly. Giving a disgusted sigh, she lifted the edge of the damp sweater and ruffled it slightly, trying to let the night air cool down her clammy body. A shower was definitely in order.

All through her shower and later while she changed into laced-edged pajamas, Robin's mind kept returning to the now sleeping man and her own reactions to him. Where had he come from? What was he doing in the area? He was hardly dressed for tramping through the woods. And what about herself? Why couldn't she make up her mind? Should she be afraid of him? He was certainly big enough and strong enough to hurt her. Sighing, Robin shook her head, chasing away her erratic thoughts as she put on the matching robe. Perhaps she ought to go and check on him once more.

He had moved into the middle of the bed, pulling the quilts askew. Robin stood in the doorway, hesitating briefly before she moved forward to smooth them back

74

into place. When she straightened up she noticed that he was awake. Her face felt stiff and frozen as she watched him uncertainly.

Nick lay silently, studying her puzzledly.

Uneasy under his intent regard, Robin offered a tentative if somewhat wary smile.

Nick made no acknowledgment of her gesture.

Robin took an uneasy step backward, then chided herself for being a coward. The man was ill, perhaps seriously so. Screwing up her courage, she took a firm step forward and peered into his face, noticing that his eyes still glittered with the remains of his fever. The dark blue eyes were glassy and glazed. Her fingers closed tightly over his wrist, searching for his pulse.

The aggressive movements of the woman in dark jade triggered latent images in Nick's confused mind. Blurred images of people holding him down, pain pricking into his head, mind-sapping drugs, and the torturous loss of control that they induced when they clouded his brain and sapped his will governed Nick's instinctive reactions. Self-preservation was essential. The woman appeared to be alone, and he could deal with her.

His powerful arm snaked out, pinning Robin's wrist in an iron grip, dragging her down onto the bed.

"Hey! Let go!" Robin's words were sharp with surprise, not wanting to accept the fact that she could be in dire trouble. Struggling to sit up, she concentrated on removing the man's shackling fingers from her wrist. "Knock it off, would you. You're hurting me!"

Dragging her back down, his large hand clamped tightly over her mouth. His eyes glittered angrily as he hissed softly. "If you make a sound, I'll kill you."

For a moment Robin was completely at a loss, completely paralyzed. Her eyes widened in shock as she took in his maniacal look. *Oh, God! He means it! What am I going to do?*

Terror welled up in her, bringing her limbs once more to life. She began to struggle in earnest, jerking this way and that. The man rolled over, pinning her to the bed. The heavy weight of one of his powerful legs fell across both of her weaker ones, preventing her from kicking free. Subdued and held captive in this manner, Robin's free hand tore at the man's wrist, trying to drag it away from her mouth. She felt the iron strength of his fingers increase, pressing harder, grinding her lips into her teeth. She tasted blood in her mouth and almost panicked. She was suffocating! Choking!

Jerking her head back away from the pressure of his hand, Robin found herself in an excellent position to retaliate. Her teeth sank into the side of his hand, only to have it snatched away before she could do any permanent damage.

Nick shifted his grip with lightning speed and captured her free hand, pinning it with its mate behind her back. He cursed softly at the pain in his hand as he laid it heavily around her throat. "If you know what's good for you, you'll keep quiet!" he commanded. "I won't tell you again."

Robin sobbed in fear and pain. Her arms ached from his brutal hold. With both her wrists captured in his iron-hard fist, and held fast behind the small of her back, Robin was forced to arch painfully. The heavy weight of his thighs ground her hips into the unyielding mattress; her breasts were crushed against his mountainous chest. For once in her life Robin was forced to acknowledge just how small and helpless a woman could be when held at the mercy of an angry man. Yet, still, in spite of her fears—or perhaps because of them—she continued to writhe, trying to struggle free. Tears choked in her throat and flooded her eyes, but she held them back, knowing that they would do her no good. She did not want to appear vulnerable. She did not want him to know just how helpless and frightened she was, but it could not be helped.

Her breathing was ragged and loud in her own ears, yet she remained mute, mindful of his warning. She could tell from the way his fingers closed around her throat that he was serious—deadly serious. Screaming for help would do her no good. There was no one who could have heard her anyway. They were alone in the valley, cut off from the world.

The man's lithe body rose to move over hers. Rough hands with strong, hurtful, probing fingers searched her body, leaving bruises wherever they touched her. Robin was shivering with terror and fear. She had to get away! She had to!

Making one last monumental effort, Robin jerked one hand free of the man's punishing hold. Her hand closed in a tight fist and she aimed for the man's face, but he shifted suddenly and the blow glanced harmlessly off his shoulder. "Damn you!" she choked on a whisper, fearful of inciting further reprisals on his part. "Let me go! I never hurt you."

Nick had to lean close to catch her words.

Robin shrank back, her eyes widening with alarm as the heavily bearded face came closer, almost touching hers. She could feel the heat of his body and see the pores of his skin. She bit her lips in an effort to hold back her tears. Would this nightmare never end?

"Who are you? Your name," he snarled.

"Robin." She faltered over it, torn by the terror of her emotions.

Nick studied her features, carefully taking in the bruised and swollen lips, the tear-filled eyes, the tousled hair. His grip loosened slightly.

"Did Liz send you?" he grated hoarsely.

What should she say? Who was this Liz? He had mentioned her often during his delirium. When he spoke of her his voice had been more gentle. Robin took a deep breath and prayed that she would make the right choice. "Yes."

Nicholas eyed her cautiously, reluctant to release her, fearing deceit. His voice was deep with suspicion. "Are you sure Liz sent you?"

Sensing that his capitulation might be at hand, Robin grasped at the chance for freedom. "Yes. Really. Liz sent me. Honestly."

Nick loosened his grip slowly, as if reluctant to let her go, and although he moved a short distance away from her, he remained close enough to grab her if she tried to get off the bed and run.

He was watching her again with that unfathomable look in his cobalt eyes. Drawing a shaky breath, Robin attempted to sit up. The hand that touched her shoulder was heavy and strong as it held her to the mattress. Swallowing down her fears, Robin made no further attempt to leave. She knew the man was waiting, ready to spring. She did not want to lose what little ground she had gained by indulging in what would undoubtedly be an abortive attempt for freedom. She lay still, trying to gain control of her seething emotions, trying to calm her fears. She could feel the cool sheets beneath her and the warm body of the man who lay beside her. She drew an unsteady breath.

Nick reached out and brushed a long strand of brown hair away from her face. Robin closed her eyes in silent prayer.

A few moist tendrils clung damply to his long fingers. He smoothed them back into place, taking pleasure in the silky feel of her hair. It reached almost to her waist. He gathered a bunch of it up, pulling it to him, touching it to his face. He had never known a woman whose hair was

78

so long that it lay thick and full enough to fill his hand and still cascade down over his arm. It felt soft and clean, smelling faintly of flowers and herbs. He breathed in its delicate scent.

His words held a mixture of arrogant assumption and surprised wonder. "You really don't mind that I messed up your hair, do you?"

Robin shook her head, unsure of what she was being asked. Her heart was pounding loudly in her ears. His words had been barely audible over its beat.

Nick's hand continued its exploratory path. Smoothing the tendrils with rough hands, he brushed the silky pelt down the length of her back, following the line of her spine. Then once again, his hand under the long brown hair, he stroked her gently, playing on each vertebra. When his fingers rested against the last one, he cupped her bottom and pulled her toward him on the large bed.

Robin couldn't repress the shudder that shook her slender frame. The man seemed no more rational now than he had been a few minutes earlier, but he was nowhere near as angry. Perhaps if she was firm and determined . . . She put both of her hands against his bare chest and pushed him away, her eyes wide and more appealing than she knew. "No. I don't want to be touched."

Nick returned his hand to her hair, smoothing it, stroking it gently. His frown was thoughtful. The slender woman's behavior was odd. She seemed almost frightened. "I thought you said Liz sent you?"

Robin closed her eyes and turned her face away from him. Although she was still frightened, she was no longer in terror for her life. Yet she had a feeling that if she was not careful, her lies might plunge her into even deeper trouble. Who was this Liz he spoke of? A procurer? If she agreed again, would she find herself in a different kind of trouble?

Nick's voice by her ear was softly coaxing. "Don't you want me to make love to you?"

Color mantled Robin's cheeks. She shook her head, answering his question even before it was finished. "No."

Nick sighed. That was really too bad. He would have enjoyed pleasuring her. "All right. Turn over on your side."

Warily Robin complied, turning her back to him. The arms that reached around her and pulled her resisting form to him were strong. Her back was sheltered against a sinewy chest, yet she felt no comfort in the embrace. When she placed her hands over his wrists, trying to free herself, he ignored her, using his larger hands to pull her down firmly onto his lap. His strong knees tucked behind hers, causing her to feel the tough muscles of his legs through the silky fabric of her pajamas and robe. One arm slid under her waist and gathered her close, then slipped across her stomach to rest lightly on her hipbone.

Robin jerked spasmodically when his right hand tucked a loose strand of hair behind her ear. Would it be best if she tried to struggle free? Or try and talk her way out?

Before she could make up her mind, she felt him run his hand down the length of her arm and cup her elbow. As he leaned forward, his lips brushed against her ear and his breath stirred the tendrils near her face. His bearded jaw touched her cheek, sending a different kind of shiver down her spine to rest churningly in the pit of her stomach.

"Liz was wrong. You're beautiful. You have beautiful green eyes too. Cat eyes." His words thickened and slurred with each sentence. "I like cats. I like you."

Her breath arrested in her throat, Robin lay still and tense. He sounded almost drugged. If he passed out again, perhaps she could get away.

After a moment his hand left her elbow and reached inside her robe that had opened during their struggles. His fingers were warm as they probed beneath it. His light touch burned her flesh, sending an additional tremor down the length of her spine. The strong hand moved sensuously over her rib cage, memorizing each bone as his fingers moved to cup one firmly rounded breast through the fabric of her lacy pajama top.

Robin gasped, shocked by his touch. No one had touched her in quite that knowing manner—no one since Randy. Jerking stiffly, she tried to shrink inward, tried to withdraw from the male presence that surrounded her on all sides.

"Relax," he muttered sleepily as his fingers squeezed gently over the pulsing mound beneath them. "You don't have to be afraid anymore. I'll take care of you now."

Her mind in a turmoil, Robin lay quiet yet rigid in his embrace, not understanding his well-meant reassurance. How strange that only moments before he was threatening to hurt her and now—now he was promising her protection. She could not bring herself to reconcile the two opposite images of the dark-bearded man.

Robin waited for a long time, trying to form a plan of escape. She knew to the second when the man fell asleep, yet she watched the minute hand of the illuminated alarm clock complete one whole cycle before she tried to release herself from his hold. Her actions were futile. When Nick felt her delicate movements, his arms tightened and his hands moved knowledgeably. One probed beneath her pajamas to rest warmly against her waist. The other cupped the flesh of her breast. Robin gasped at the involuntary and unwanted reaction of her traitorous body when his fingers brushed against the rosy peak.

"Lie still, woman," Nick murmured softly, still half asleep. "No one can hurt you while I hold you."

Unable to do otherwise, Robin did as she was bid. Shivering with a cold that was brought on by two kinds of fear

81

and a welter of confused thoughts, she reached for the tangled covers and pulled them close, seeking their warmth to stop her chills. Eventually the warmth of the covers and the man's body transferred itself to hers. At last the events of the long day took their toll. Slowly her mind began to wind down and her body began to relax as each individual muscle unknotted. Her eyes grew heavy; her tension eased away. She began to feel warm. Protected. Her exhausted mind drifted, forgetting its fears, remembering only the soft, coaxing reassurance in the husky voice of her self-appointed guardian. At last she slept.

CHAPTER SEVEN

When Nicholas Armstrong woke, the winter sun was high in the intensely blue sky. His mind was clear at last from the combined effects of the drugs and his fevered exhaustion. He had slept deeply and now he woke feeling utterly at peace with his surroundings.

The first thing his eyes saw was a panoramic view of craggy snow-capped mountains. A little more alert but still drowsy, Nick's eyes took stock of the room where he lay and the young woman who nestled against his shoulder. A tiny frown etched his brow as he tried to remember her name—Robin.

Her light weight was warm and comforting. He cradled her petite form in his arms, enjoying the scent of her warm, feminine body, the silken luxury of her cinnamon hair, and the feel of her womanly curves against his skin.

Shifting in the bed, Nick pushed the pillows behind his back so that he half sat. Although the woman stirred at his movements, she did not wake. However, she did snuggle closer and her arm tightened along his waist.

His fingers tangling softly in Robin's hair, Nick remembered the last few hellish days. They had been a nightmare's fog that had given him only bits and pieces of his actions. Confused memories of men and women holding him down, threatening him, hurting him, soothing him, and comforting him. He could remember days of drug-induced stupors and moments of burning agony of mind and soul. There were also vague recollections of traveling by plane, the stormy weather, the jarring crash, and the bodies of men crowding his mind. He remembered the endless miles of snow-covered mountains and forests. And foggy fantasies of ice castles in the snow.

This woman who lay so trustingly in his arms was no easier to remember. Pictures flitted from various parts of his brain to tease him. Pictures of her frightened and angry. Pictures of her features incredibly softened with concern and compassion.

Nick moved his foot to touch against her instep, measuring her height against the length of his body. She barely came up to the center of his chest. She was so tiny in comparison to himself that he felt protective.

The thought made him smile. Liz had been right. It was a male desire to want to play the role of a macho protector. This woman seemed like a trusting child, sleeping peacefully in his arms.

No, not a child, Nick amended silently. He studied her shape thoughtfully, allowing his hands to follow the path of discovery his eyes had made. She moved restlessly under his touch. She was what in olden days might have been termed a pocket Venus. She was petite, but her curves were full and shapely. She had an earthy naturalness that was refreshing in comparison to the svelte sophistication of the women he usually dated. Her eyes were long and narrow, tilting slightly upward at the end. Her thick brows were delicately arched. Her features, daintily feline as she curled comfortably into his side, her lashes long and dark. Nick smiled with a vague recollection of jade green cat eyes.

Her dark jade robe and pajamas clung to her curving hips and flat stomach. Her waist was so tiny that Nick felt that it could be spanned by his two hands. He laid the fingers of one hand experimentally on her waist. The tips of his long fingers curled around her waist and laid flat along her back. They reached well past the middle of her spine. Nick felt gratified that his estimate had been correct.

A tantalizing glimpse of a swelling curve caught his attention. The lacy jacket rested against her creamy complexion and what little he could see of her breast was firm and satiny.

Her cheeks were flushed with sleep. Her parted lips glistened moistly red over small even teeth. The luxurious length of her cinnamon-colored hair lay spread across his arm on the pale green pillows. He stroked it softly, enjoying again its silky texture.

Robin stirred, moaning softly in her sleep.

Nick touched her, lightly stroking her. Delighting in the feather-light weight of her arm around his middle. He lay still for a few minutes more, watching her sleep. This place suited her. Her face was as clear and open as the valley and the mountains around them. He felt at home and at peace. Nothing about her or the room had the bustling feel of the city. The decor was modern but tastefully chosen to enhance the naturalness of the setting. Just as the solitary gold chain she wore enhanced the woman's own natural beauty.

Robin stirred a couple of times before finally waking. The persistent *thump-thump* of something warm by her ear finally roused her, pulling away the last curtain of sleep. Robin stretched sensually against the hard, warm surface next to her. Her fingers brushed across a springy

85

mat of fiber. She buried her fingers in its texture and encountered a solid surface of warm flesh.

Robin's body jerked. Her eyes flew open. Her head tilted back. Her jade eyes widened with shock. She remembered! Fear returned in a rush, paralyzing the muscles of her throat.

Dark blue eyes watched her with amused concern, and something else that lurked deep within their depths.

Nick gently stroked her arm, trying to soothe her fright. His fingers moved lightly to her hair, playing with the soft tendrils. Slowly, seductively, his fingers drifted down her back, tracing the curving line of her spine. When they reached the small of her back he shifted, gathering her to him, letting her feel the muscles of his powerful thighs. His cobalt eyes never left her jade ones.

Robin's breath caught sharply in her throat and her eyes dilated widely as she tried to decide on the best course of action open to her. Should she fight? Or try to talk to him? Or simply accept his kisses. *Oh, Lord! I'm as crazy as he is! This has got to stop!*

Before Robin could utter a word, Nick's eyes darkened and he lowered his bearded face to taste her parted lips. Her mouth was pliant beneath his—moist and sweet. The warmth of her lips aroused a protectiveness and a passion in him as had no other woman. Nick deepened his kiss, letting her feel the edge of his rising passion.

Robin's fingers tightened unconsciously over his broad shoulders before she pushed him away, but she couldn't find her voice to strengthen her denial. The probing tongue that had invaded her reluctantly retreated.

Nick's gaze was somber, trying to decide just what kind of game she was playing. His eyes held speculation as he watched a rosy blush rise to her cheeks. Brows knit to show his confusion, his thumb traced the line of her jaw, moving upward to her wide, generous mouth. He brushed gently at her full lower lip, pushing her lips apart, to rest the ball of his thumb against her even white teeth. When Robin's tongue darted nervously across his teeth, accidentally touching the tip of his finger, Nick's eyes darkened dramatically. He lowered his head again, intent on capturing the fleeting movement.

Robin accepted his kiss mutely this time, offering no resistance. When he lifted his head, her eyes were bruised and filled with confusion and a hint of fear.

Nick moved his hand down to stroke the delicate column of her throat, wanting to ease away her uncertainties. Following the outline of the V neck of her jacket to the softly scented valley between her breasts, he pushed the top aside and rested his hand against her heart. It pounded like a wild thing beneath his fingers. His knuckles brushed roughly against the swelling curve of her creamy flesh. Robin tried to stifle a deep whimper when he held one taut breast in his hand. Her teeth bit deeply into her lower lip, drawing blood. Again Nick lowered his head, kissing her long and longingly.

Robin could not understand this weaknesss in herself. This man, this bearded, bedraggled stranger meant to seduce her, to touch her in a way that no one since Randy had, so long ago. Yet, she could make no attempt to stop him.

It was not just her fear that held her back. Her flesh burned at his touch. The soft scratchy quality of his probing kisses caused her clamoring senses to swim headily. Robin feared his possession, yet seemed powerless to prevent it. The touch of his lips, the feel of his warm hands on her vulnerable flesh, enflamed her own senses and weakened her. Last night she feared his rage, this morning his passion.

What was happening to her? How could she even think of responding to someone as unknown and unnerving as this—this stranger? She had known Randy all her life. She had loved him dearly and completely—and yet, even with him, she had not been subject to this overwhelming inability to control her own destiny.

Robin shivered with the icy-hot feelings he aroused in her when his tongue traced around the hardening peak of her breast. Her small hands clenched into tight fists at her side, her nails cutting deeply into her palms when his teeth nipped sensuously and joined his tongue in its tasting of her flesh. She was struggling to regain some of her lost sanity, her breath labored and uneven. Her body trembled as if with ague beneath the sensual onslaught.

Nick slipped her robe off her shoulders and then the lace-edged jacket. His hand moved over her breasts and Robin felt swamped by the emotions his touch ignited in her. His consuming passion overwhelmed her. Mentally she feared his touch, but her body had a mind of its own, submitting willingly to his ardor. Robin moaned deeply, unable to offer even token resistance.

His strong fingers pushed the top aside and began to brush tantalizingly along her ribs. His tongue laved a path to her navel. The scratchy soft feel of his beard caused her stomach muscles to cramp achingly. When his tongue probed her navel, sanity returned at last in a rushing roar. Her body jerked rigidly. Robin put her hands on his shoulders and pushed him away. Her fingernails bit into his brawny shoulders, leaving small crescent-shaped wounds.

Nick felt her withdrawal instantly, causing him pain that was mental as well as physical. Her body had been so attuned to his, its responses had echoed his own. It took him a few minutes to regain his own control. His breath came in quick, uneven gasps, eventually taking on a more normal rhythm. Several minutes passed before he could lift his heavy body off her soft one. Cool air rushed in,

touching their burning skin, leaving Robin shivering uncontrollably.

"What's wrong, Snow Queen?" Nick's voice was tender, husky, refusing to inflict her with the frustration he
was feeling at her refusal.

Robin's voice was choked, her fear tangible. "Are you
going to hurt me?"

Nick's shock was total. It had never occurred to him
that she might view his actions as being punitive. His voice
was gruff with denial. "No. Never."

She believed him. Relief swept over her, yet the swift
release of tension left her trembling visibly. Nick cradled
her shaking body against his lithe frame.

While he was cuddling her in his arms, Nick noticed for
the first time a number of yellowish-purple smudges that
dotted her partially bared torso and arms. There was no
doubt that the marks on her body had been caused by him.
He cursed the blank spots of his memory. There was much
he needed to know about his relationship with this brown-
haired woman. He had assumed that because she had lain
nestled in his embrace this morning when he woke and
found her sharing the wide bed, that she had been a willing
participant in whatever had taken place. Her subsequent
actions had disabused him of that notion. Her obvious
relief indicated that far from being a willing participant,
she had felt herself coerced and threatened into remaining
compliant beneath his touch.

Eventually her tremblings subsided under his gentle
ministrations. Her body lost some of its rigidity and
became supple and pliant, molding itself to the warmth of
his. She lay quietly within his hold, her body subcon-
sciously accepting his companionship that her conscious
mind refused to acknowledge. After a while, Robin inched
slowly and cautiously away from him. She was astonish-

ingly aware of the tall man who held her treacherous body.

"Where are you going, Snow Queen?" His baritone was low and slightly husky.

Robin hesitated, trying to judge whether or not she would be allowed to leave. Nick made no move to force her to remain. A fleeting smile flickered nervously across her face, her jade-colored eyes darkly serious.

Nick felt gripped with remorse. She was still in fear of him—and apparently with just cause.

"Did I—" He faltered. A long finger traced a particularly vicious purple bruise on her shoulder. "Did I do that to you?"

"Yes." Her voice was low. Robin bit her lip while fear danced in her eyes, remembering the time when it had reigned supreme throughout her slight frame.

Nicholas forced himself to continue his interrogation. "Did I—" Again he hesitated. He needed the reassurance, the solace of her body beneath his touch before he could go on. His hands tenderly drew the lace-edged jacket over her shoulders. He eased the robe over the top, drawing it together to cover her breasts. His hand stroked her hair away from her pale white face.

"Did I hurt you last night?" His voice was low, begging for her to deny it.

"No." Her eyes were watchful, wary.

"Thank God!" Nick's response was fervent. He rested his chin on the top of her head, holding her tight against his own body. A tremor passed through him.

Tentatively a pale white hand fluttered near him. Robin comforted him, touching him lightly, still a little filled with awe and fear. She did not really pay attention to the words she uttered. She only wanted to reassure and comfort this strangely distraught man.

Nick looked deep into her eyes, unhappily aware of the

answer to his question. "Could you have forgiven me if I had?"

Robin looked away, refusing to perjure herself.

Nick released her. He looked around the room, spotting his clothes neatly stacked in a chair by the opposite side of the bed. He got up and swiftly pulled on his jeans and slipped into the woolen shirt.

Robin sat up in the middle of the bed, holding her robe against her. Her legs were still tangled in the sheets. Nick moved back over to the bed and sat down on its edge by her feet. One large hand thrust through his jet black hair while the other fumbled with the buttons of his shirt. He lowered his hand to rest on her knee, waiting until she raised her gaze to his.

"Do you have a telephone? I'd like to let my folks know where I am."

Robin shook her head. "The line's dead."

"Can I get to another place where there is one?"

"Not easily. It will take us most of the day just to dig ourselves out. By the time we do, it will be too dark to go down the mountain. We're about thirty or so miles from the nearest place."

Nick looked surprised. "You live here all alone?"

"Not usually. But for the moment I do." Robin shifted uncomfortably on the bed. She was nervous about remaining in the bedroom with him.

Nick read her nervousness and understood it. "Do you think you could fix us some breakfast?"

Relieved, Robin rose rapidly to her feet, feeling dwarfed by his bulk as he, too, rose. "Sure, come on into the kitchen. It's at the far end of the hall. I'll fix you some toast and a poached egg. I think what I fed you last night was a little too heavy."

Nick followed her out of the bedroom. At the door he stopped abruptly. His eyes scanned the glass-enclosed hall. It reminded him more of a breezeway than a typical hall. A patio area in a classical Spanish style lay on the other side of the windows. It was filled with drifts of snow. Through the windows on the far side he could see the open area of a book-lined study, a closed area, a large front room, a dining room, and at the far end—near the kitchen where they were headed—an indoor garden.

"I didn't dream it?" His voice was questioning.

Robin turned to see what he was looking at. When she realized that he referred to the design of the house she laughed lightly and naturally.

"It affects everyone like that at first. My dad designed it for my mother. She wanted to be as close to nature as possible. This way, with all the glass and open spaces, you feel that you're in the forest—a part of it.

"It's fantastic," she continued. "I've lived here for four years now. I love it. I don't think that I could ever leave it to go back to the city for more than a few weeks at a time. I remember when I was little my parents and I used to live for vacations and summers so that we could get back here."

Nick nodded, taking in the fantastic view of the Rockies that presented itself on all sides. "I could see why. It certainly is spectacular. These mountains—I've never seen anything like them."

Robin continued to lead the way into the kitchen, motioning Nick to sit down.

"I know. They are magnificent. I think that's what I like best about Colorado," she continued. "We have three completly different types of topography. The Great Plains to the east, the Rocky Mountains here, and the plateaus. It's like having the best of all worlds in my own backyard."

Nick was incredulous. "Colorado? Are you telling me I'm in Colorado?"

92

Robin was astounded. "Well, of course you are. Where did you think you were?"

Nick shrugged, still not taking it all in. "I don't know. I guess I just didn't stop to think about it. I knew I wasn't near home, but I never expected—Colorado?" He just had to question it again.

Robin nodded solemly.

Nicholas Armstrong took a good look around him. He was perplexed. He studied the valley and the mountains outside the kitchen windows.

"Yes," he muttered softly to himself, "I guess it would have to be one of the Rocky Mountain states at that." These mountains were taller than any he had ever seen east of the Mississippi River. The fact that they were not completely covered with deciduous trees or conifers should have told him that earlier. The timberline was a dead giveaway.

Robin's low contralto broke into his reverie. "How is it that you ended up here?"

Nick shrugged again. "It's a long story."

Robin turned sharply away, feeling snubbed. She moved to the refrigerator and took out a carton of eggs and a stick of butter. Nick watched her jerky movements as she filled a Teflon pan with water and set it on the stove with a snap. He intercepted her on the way to the toaster. His hands felt heavy on her shoulders. He bent to peer straight into her eyes.

"I am not trying to be difficult or secretive," he explained. "It is a long story. And parts of it—well, I haven't got it all sorted out in my mind yet."

"I'm sorry." Robin moved uneasily beneath his grasp, still not wholly convinced. "It's just—"

"I know. I appear one day on your doorstep and ask you to take me on faith. The circumstances are bizarre to say the least." His voice was cajoling.

93

Robin hesitated briefly, then capitulated, responding to his unasked plea for time. "Bizarre isn't the half of it. I found you on my sofa on Christmas morning."

Nick was flabbergasted. "On your—" He broke off abruptly. "Christmas? It's Christmas?"

Now it was Robin's turn to be astonished. "Didn't you know that it was Christmas either?"

Nick shook his head slowly. He sank into a chair by the kitchen table. "Oh, God! I'll bet my family and friends think I'm dead."

Robin was confused, but she understood his anguish and placed a sympathetic hand on his shoulder. "I am sorry. We really can't get through today and we probably won't be able to for a couple of days, to be perfectly honest.

"I know what it's like to worry about your family. My mom and dad are in St. Louis for a few months. The waiting can be hell, but you really will have to wait. If we aren't careful getting down the mountain, we could get killed."

She looked around the valley. "It's really nice today. The wind isn't blowing or anything. But the weather reports indicate that it will probably start blowing tomorrow, and in addition more snow is expected off and on until after the first of the new year. Today is the twenty-sixth. If the wind and the snow do come, they'll last until the twenty-eighth or ninth for sure. It will take us a full day to dig out the garage. The snowmobiles are in good shape, but we would need to be prepared with extra clothing and rations in case something went wrong. And we would both have to go down. You don't know the trails and the snowplows won't come up here. We are well and truly off the beaten track.

"However, it might all not be so bad. Depending on where the lines are down, the telephone could be back in

94

service by tonight or tomorrow. And the rangers do drop by here occasionally—just to check up on us and make sure that we're all right. If they were to come by before we could get out, they would take a message to your family."

Nick put his arms around her waist, holding her loosely, drawing comfort from her body. His head rested against her breast.

"I guess I don't have much choice, do I?"

Robin touched the wavy black locks lightly. "I guess you don't."

CHAPTER EIGHT

By the time breakfast was over, Nick was feeling much better. Robin urged him to lie down again, but Nick insisted that he wanted to clean up first.

"You can use my parents' room while you are here."

Robin led him back to the room where he had spent the night. She eyed him contemplatively before turning to flick through one half of the large closet.

"Here, you can change into these." She handed him a pair of jeans. "Socks and underwear are in the top left-hand side of the dresser."

"Thanks."

"I'm afraid you'll have to make due with your own shirt. You are about the same height and build as my dad, but your shoulders are much wider. I don't think any of his shirts will fit you."

Nick sneezed.

"The bathroom is through that door. There are some cold tablets in the medicine cabinet. You may want to take a couple to ward off any germs that you might have picked up. Leave the door unlocked in case you fall or need any help."

Nick padded through the door Robin had indicated and found himself in a large roomy bathroom. A fiber glass tub with a separate shower filled one side of the pale blue wall. Musing that this must be the master bedroom's private bath, Nick turned on the spray and stepped beneath the pulsing jets. It was going to feel good to be clean again. Clean all over. He reached for the soap-on-a-rope that hung from the shower caddy. Sniffing at its pleasant odor, he grunted.

"Brut. I'll bet that's exactly what the Snow Queen thinks I am."

He shrugged dismissively and got down to the business of lathering up. When he finished rinsing he found a bottle of shampoo and washed his hair too. The shampoo stung his scalp when it entered the cut and Nick swore softly, quickly finishing washing and rinsing his head. Finished, he turned off the shower and stepped out of the tub. He grabbed the first towel he saw and wrapped it tightly around his lean hips, not even realizing that the blue of the towel matched exactly the blue of his eyes.

Nick walked to the mirrors that lined one side of the bath. He stopped, startled at his own reflection. A two-week growth of beard had changed his normally open face astonishingly. He looked like a ruffian—a barbarian. It was a wonder she hadn't called the police. Even his own father would not have recognized him.

Nick automatically reached for the electric razor, then stayed his hand. *Not being recognized . . . that could have certain advantages.* He began searching through the drawers that lined the cabinet until he found a pair of scissors. He trimmed the wild growth of his beard to a more presentable form, but he did not remove it.

A light tap on the door heralded Robin's sweet contralto. "Are you alive in there?"

Nick flung open the door, still clad only in the towel that had slipped low around his hips. Nick swiftly smothered a grin as she backed hastily away, a furious blush mantling her cheeks.

"You were so long in there, I wondered—"

"If I fell asleep in the tub? No, I'm fine. Give me a minute and I'll be right with you." His fingers went to the knot of the blue towel, toying with it, unable to prevent himself from teasing.

Robin fled, cursing her idiotic behavior. She had been married for three years, hadn't she?

Twin devils of teasing torment danced in Nick's cobalt eyes. It was a novel experience for him. The women he knew usually eyed his masculine form with an assessment that was as blatant as his own had been. She seemed almost too innocent to be for real. She was young, all right—but not that young. Nick grabbed his borrowed jeans and pulled them on thoughtfully. He wanted to know more about this place before he answered too many of her questions. It was possible that this was just another trick.

The first thing Nicholas noticed on entering the front room was that Robin had changed her pajamas and robe. She now wore a pair of snug blue jeans and a soft angora sweater. The second thing that he noticed was how closely the fluffy sweater outlined her very feminine curves. Its short sleeves revealed a pair of nicely rounded arms of pale cream. Her long cinnamon hair had been bundled up at the back of her head. The column of her neck appeared fragile, almost too delicate to support the weight of the masses of long curls. Her back was to him, and when she leaned over to plump one of the crewel pillows, the fabric of her snug jeans tightened, affording him an excellent view of her derriere. The third thing that Nick noticed was that that particular derriere was extremely cute and sexy —even when she straightened.

Nick sneezed.

Robin turned, hands on hips. A slight scowl marred her delicate features. She was not really a beautiful woman, but her looks were charming. Thick brows arched delicately over thick cinnamon-colored lashes surrounding the deep pools of jade. Nick was amused by his flight of fancy.

Unaware of his thoughts, Robin frowned at him. "You sound like you're catching something. I really think you ought to spend the day in bed."

Nick shook his head firmly. "No. I'm too restless to go back to sleep. Besides, I've lost too many days already to want to lose any more."

"Well, at least you can get under that quilt."

Nick padded over to the couch, sneezing twice on the way. Robin left the room as he unfolded the large handmade quilt. Sighing, he sank down on the sofa and looked out the floor-to-ceiling windows that opened up onto the forest surrounding the glass house.

A box of Kleenex dropped down beside him. Nicholas raised his eyes to see Robin standing behind him on the slate that served as a floor for the raised hallway. The flooring was level with his shoulder, so that Nicholas could reach out one large hand and catch her slender ankle in his grasp. The skin beneath his fingers felt like velvet.

Robin made no attempt to move away. She was still somewhat leery of this stranger, but she realized that like the sleek cat he so resembled, he was a hunter by nature. To flee would invite pursuit.

"Did you take any medicine earlier?"

Nick released her ankle in order to run one frost-reddened hand through his black hair. "A couple of aspirin. I'll be all right. It's just a chill."

He tucked the quilt more securely around his long length and stretched his legs out, taking up more than three-quarters of the six-foot couch, Robin noted with some amusement.

"Just exactly where is this place anyway?"

Robin walked down the steps by the dining room and then came closer to curl up on the far end of the couch. The sun glinted gold on the fine mesh of the necklace at her throat. She took her time before answering.

"This valley is located about thirty or so miles northeast of Rifle, Colorado. We are located pretty high up in the White River Forest. Actually I suppose we might be closer to Buford or New Castle, as the crow flies, but our road connects up with the main road into Rifle about twenty miles down."

Nick watched her nimble fingers push the crewel thread through the linen she had brought back with her. The delicate movements of her hands were riveting. He had thought that embroidery was a forgotten art.

"I'm afraid my ignorance is showing. I've never heard of Rifle."

Robin shrugged. Rifle was small enough that most people wouldn't have heard of it. "It's a medium-size city in the western half of the state and pretty much on the same level as Denver on a map. The valley, here, is about a hundred and fifty miles west of Denver and only about a hundred or so miles from the Utah border. I've an atlas in the study. Would you like me to go in and find it?"

"No, not just now." Nick wanted to keep her talking. He was enjoying the low, melodious quality of her voice. "I have an idea of where we're located now. Just go on with your sewing. What is it anyway?"

Robin smoothed the fabric out across her lap and his extended legs. "It's a design for a family tree."

Nick grunted. "Looks complicated."

"No." Robin looked straight into his dark eyes. "Probably even less complicated than how you managed to get here." She had every intention of hearing whatever tale he told. Occasionally a tourist managed to get lost on the winding roads that laced their way through the mountains, but it was usually in the summer and no one had ever arrived on foot before. Until he told her more, she would remain wary. *Besides,* she told herself, *the very ease with which he made himself at home was unnerving, to say the least.*

Nick sent her an utterly beguiling smile. "I couldn't say," His voice was rich with charm. "I've never tried my hand at anything like that. Is it for your parents?"

Robin's tongue traced the edge of her upper teeth and tried not to let her shoulders stiffen with the tension that she felt returning. "Not exactly." Her jade eyes affirmed her resolve as one brow arched in polite inquiry. "You never did say how you came to be here."

"I saw the house from up on the bluff. Do you—"

Robin made no attempt to hide her frown of impatience. It was deep and dark and drew her brows together over her eyes and nose. "For someone who asks a lot of questions, you sure don't answer many."

Nick's gaze was speculative and every bit as wary as hers. He really didn't want to explain himself. Too much was still unanswered in his own mind. The events of the past couple of weeks had enforced the idea that he needed to rely solely upon himself. The fact that she had not called the police—or at least some help—to aid her when she found a stranger in her house, was suspicious. It crossed his mind that there was always the possibility that she was somehow involved in what had transpired.

Nick scrutinized her face openly. Innocence looked back. He shook his head. He was too suspicious. It was highly unlikely that she was involved. On the other hand, if someone did come looking for him, it might prove dangerous for her to know too much.

Robin stood swiftly and paced to the glass windows, staring out into the snow-covered forest. After a few moments she came back and gathered up her sewing materials.

"Keep your damn secrets." Robin turned to flounce away.

The hard hand that snaked out to capture her wrist was strong, very strong. But Nick did not use his strength against her. Instead, his other hand coaxed her into releasing the materials she had gathered up. Once the linen, thread, needles, and scissors had been relinquished to the coffee table, he asked her softly, "Are you really sure you want to know? It could be dangerous."

"Dangerous?" Robin was taken aback. "Are you—" Her eyes widened at the possibility. "Are you in some kind of trouble?"

"Not with the police." Nick assured her.

"Well, then, who?"

"I'm not exactly sure."

"This is ridiculous." Robin snatched her wrist from his fingers and knelt to pick up her sewing.

His large hands clamped down over her angora-covered shoulders. His fingers automatically burrowed sensuously into its softness. His thumbs began to trace the line of her collarbone to the hollow at the base of her throat, toying with the gold chain that circled her neck. Robin's startled gasp of surprise drew his attention to ripe red lips. Exerting pressure on her shoulder, Nick drew her closer.

A small but firm, pink-tipped hand anchored itself in

102

the center of his chest, exerting an equal but contrary pressure of its own.

"I bet you keep your wife barefoot and pregnant too."

Amusement took over his emotions. Nick recognized the statement for the question that it was. He released her slowly. "I'm not married, but Liz thinks I ought to be."

Liz, the procurer. Changed to Liz, the matchmaker? Possible. Plausible. Robin sat down at the far end of the couch, tucking her legs underneath her Indian-fashion. Her slender arm rested along the back of the couch and her hand played with its tree-bark-brown nap.

"I can see why, if that"—she motioned to the spot where she had been kneeling moments earlier—"is your usual approach."

This time Nick prudently ignored the questioning statement.

"Is Liz your girlfriend?"

"No, she's my best friend's wife. The three of us grew up together back in Bloomington, Illinois. After college I started a business in Chicago. Tom, that's Liz's husband, runs the fabricating end and Liz manages the accounting and office staff."

"What about you?"

Nicholas shrugged one hefty masculine shoulder. "I do most of the drafting and designing."

The silence that followed lasted several minutes, then Robin spoke diffidently. "Look, I know you don't want to talk about this—but try looking at it from my point of view. Some stranger breaks into my house—"

"I didn't break in. The door was open."

Robin waved her hand dismissively. "That's not the point. Some strange man comes into my home, passes out on my couch, scares the daylights out of me . . . Do I need to go on?"

"No, you don't need to elaborate. If I were in your

position, I would undoubtedly feel the same. In fact, I probably wouldn't have been as understanding as you've been."

He sat back, sighing. "Listen. This is kind of complicated, and I don't have all the answers myself, but I'll try to answer some of your questions. Okay?"

Robin relaxed in her position at the end of the couch and picked up her crewel embroidery again.

"Thank you. I would appreciate it." Her response was dry.

Nick muffled a laugh. "Do you always sew?"

"It's the only way to get it done. Why? Does it bother you? I can do this and listen too."

"No, it's just so unusual."

Seeing her inquiring glance, he continued. "You appear to be busy every minute yet it isn't a restless kind of activity. Instead"—he shrugged—"I don't know. At least it is a nice change from fidgeting."

"And it provides you with an excellent opportunity to change the subject. Right?" She mocked him with a trace of sarcasm.

Nick sighed. Robin was determined to get the full story. "I had been out to eat with the rest of the people I work with. It was our annual Christmas party on a Friday about two weeks before Christmas. We had gone to the Khyber. When I got home it turned out to be earlier than I had expected, so I decided to stay up and get some packing done. I was going to go home the next day for the holidays. My father still lives back in Bloomington, with Jill."

Anticipating her question he added mockingly. "Jill, by the way, is my stepmother."

As the silence lengthened Robin prodded. "And . . ."

"And nothing. Just my stepmother."

"Not—and Jill. Just—and what happened next."

Nick snorted disgustedly. "I heard someone knocking on the front door of the apartment, so I answered it. There were two men standing there. One was in a business suit and the other in a policeman's uniform. They showed me their IDs and I let them in. The older man, the one in the suit, told me that Jill had been in an accident and that my father wanted me to try to catch an earlier flight home. The other one, the officer, offered me a stiff drink—and like an idiot, I drank it."

Robin frowned. "That seems reasonable enough."

"Not if it is drugged." Nick was staring into Robin's eyes. The shock of surprise that slowly filled them could not have been faked. She was not involved. He continued, more at ease with her than before.

"I honestly don't remember much more than that. About the only time I wasn't drugged to the hilt was when they put me on the plane."

All Robin's attention was focused on the man in front of her. The embroidery lay forgotten in her lap. Her voice was breathless with tension. "Who were they?"

"I can't say for sure. Most of the time they spoke a foreign language. Occasionally I think I recognized a word or two—but I don't know for sure. It wasn't a language that I speak. Just one that I'd heard before.

"My company is doing some work for one of the emerging Arab nations. It might have had something to do with that. I don't know for sure. I can only guess. The people I seem to remember were dark-haired and dark-eyed, rather swarthy too." He shrugged with finality. "It is only a guess."

"You said they put you on a plane?"

Nick grunted. "Yeah. It was one of those small single-engine jobs. I was still pretty doped up, but I do remember that we stopped to refuel at least once. To be perfectly honest, I was probably flying as high as the plane right about then." Sweat broke out on his brow. "God! I don't know how the addicts stand it. It's hell not being in control of your own body."

"How long were you—"

"Until after I showed up here. In fact, today is the first time I've felt really aware of what's going on around me. However, I must have been beginning to come out of it a little just before the crash."

"Crash? You mean somebody might be out there looking for you?"

Nick shook his head. "Not from the plane. The pilot and his buddy were both dead when I left. I took one of their coats and got away from the plane. I don't know where my coat was. It's still kind of mixed up in my mind, but I remember walking around." A flick of his hand indicated the forest. "I knew what had happened, but I kept thinking that I had to get to my father's place. I just couldn't seem to deal with what was happening to me. I knew I was lost, so I just kept on walking around, trying to find someplace I knew or at least some kind of shelter. I was up on one of those outcroppings when I noticed the smoke from your chimney."

"Hmm. This place is solar-heated, so if you saw the smoke . . . Why, you must have come in just a few minutes after I went to bed. I really didn't leave all that much of a fire going."

Nick shrugged. "I guess so. Anyway, it was warm and I seem to remember finding something to drink."

Robin laughed self-consciously. "You wouldn't think a simple toast could cause so much havoc."

She continued in response to his raised eyebrow. "My parents were in St. Louis for Thanksgiving and it was pretty lonely here. I missed them terribly. When they let me know that they couldn't make it home for Christmas either I decided to do Christmas up proper so that I would not feel so isolated—you know, Christmas dinner, the tree, decorations, the whole bit. I thought that I might not be so depressed. It would make it more like they were here, but maybe just in another room. I thought I could pretend anyway."

Noticing his perplexed scowl, Robin finished hurriedly. "Ever since I can remember, my family has toasted the Christmas season with my dad's best whiskey on Christmas Eve. Since I don't really care for the taste of whiskey, I didn't finish my drink. When I came in the next morning and saw that the glass was empty . . ." A slow, teasing smile spread over her delicate features. "Well, you would have had to have been there to understand."

Nick began laughing as comprehension dawned. "What happened next?"

She pleated the cloth in her lap and then met his inquiring look with a half defiant, half guilty one of her own. "First I went to the kitchen and got a sharp knife."

At his startled oath Robin lashed out angrily. "What would you have done? Here I am—alone in this house. The weather was awful. One of the worst winter storms of the season. Even if I had called the sheriff he couldn't have sent anyone until the storm let up. It would have been hours at the very least. And by then it might have been too late."

"You little fool!" Nick was surprised by his own anger. "Don't you know that a man—any man—could take the knife away in a minute and use it against you?"

"What would you have me do?" Robin's temper flared. "Give up without a struggle?"

"Wouldn't that be better than having your pretty little throat slit?" he growled.

"You can't make me believe that you would have submitted to your captors without a fight." Flinging her embroidery down on the coffee table, Robin strode to the far end of the garden room. She lowered herself angily to a wide grassy strip and stared mutinously out of the window.

Nick swore heartily and thoroughly. Hastily he followed her into the garden room. Stooping down beside her, resting on his haunches, arms hung loosely across his knees, he tried to placate her.

"I'm sorry, Snow Queen. I suppose you did the best you could under the circumstances. It's just—"

"That's big of you." She interrupted with biting sarcasm.

His hands reached out and dragged her roughly to her knees. "You stupid idiot! You could have been killed, pulling a stunt like that!"

Suddenly all the fears of the past day washed over Robin. Anger and hatred warred through her mind. "Don't you think I know that now?" she raged. "When I came back later and saw you holding that knife like you wanted to—"

"What?"

Furiously, Robin struggled free of his hold. Angrily she pushed his strong hands away from her body, her eyes snapping. "Go away! I don't want to talk to you anymore."

"Look," Nick said, "you have to tell me what happened. I don't remember any of this."

"No! Go away! Just leave me alone!"

Nick stood first, then leaned over, hauling Robin first to her feet and then high into his arms. He carried her back to the couch in the front room. Surprisingly enough, she lay passively in his arms, her arms around his neck, her bright cinnamon head resting on his brawny chest. Nick ran his hands lightly down her back and arms, holding her loosely.

Robin sighed and snuggled more comfortably into his

108

arms, realizing that he was as confused by what was happening to them as she was. Who could explain it? She certainly couldn't. All she knew was that this man felt so incredibly big and strong and protective. Robin remembered unwittingly his words from the previous evening. *You don't have to be afraid anymore. I'll take care of you.* Briefly she wondered if he remembered them too.

"When I came back with the knife"—Robin's voice was so low that Nick had to bend his head to hear her—"I took a closer look at you." She shrugged off-handedly, her head still resting against the solid warmth of his chest. "You were awfully scruffy-looking, but you had a nice face under all that hair, and you were obviously ill, so I left you alone."

"What about the knife, Snow Queen?" he persisted.

"Why do you call me that?"

Nick's grin was mocking. "Changing the subject, hmm? When I was wandering around out there, looking for some kind of shelter, I first saw this place in the moonlight. It looked like something out of a fairy tale that I'd been reading to Candy—all glitter and ice. And since you seem to be the only resident, that makes you the Snow Queen."

A sweet smile slipped across her hidden features. Not many men would admit to reading fairy tales to a child. Looking up, she dared to tease. "Candy, hmm. Don't you know any men?"

"Candy is my goddaughter."

"Sure." Robin mocked him lightly. "I hear you."

"Unh-unh. We were talking about the knife, remember?"

Robin capitulated with a grimacing shudder. "You held that knife like you knew how to use it." She sat up in his lap. "I knew then that I had been stupid to bring it."

"How in hell did I get it away from you?"

Robin looked away. This wasn't something she wanted to face just now.

"I'm waiting." Nick's words were menacing.

"Oh, shut up! When I saw how ill you were I forgot all about the knife. I put it down."

"You left it in here? You just left it with me?" His voice was harsh, filled with anger.

Robin broke free of his restraining hold, jumped up, and paced around the room. "Go to hell! I don't have to answer to you or to anyone else. Just leave me alone!"

"My God, woman! I could have been anybody. A murderer or a rapist."

She whirled, fury seething in every movement. "Don't you think I realized that? Don't you think I knew?"

Robin dropped into a nearby chair and covered her face with her hands. How dare he censure her? Her nerves felt shot, but her temper was reaching new heights.

Nick left the sofa and came to her. When his hands touched her shoulders he felt her flinch.

"Oh, God!" he groaned. "I'm not going to hurt you now."

Nick sat down on the arm of her chair and pulled her head down onto his lap. Robin put up a token resistance and then subsided, flinging her arms around his waist and holding him tight. She wanted the comfort and warmth that he offered. She had run the gamut of emotions yesterday and today. She had been independent—she had always been independent, even when Randy had been so ill. Yet now she wanted nothing more than to be cosseted. What was the matter with her? Why was she behaving so oddly? What kind of magic was there in the fingers that she felt moving softly in her hair, removing her bobby pins, and petting the strands down the length of her back.

His gentle fingers continued to thread through her hair. "Okay?"

110

Robin nodded, breathing in the pleasant odor of his soap-scented body. It felt nice lying against a man again, knowing that he wouldn't let anything hurt her. Robin's eyes drooped; the fingers against her head had a comforting, soporific feel. Her arms and legs were beginning to feel too heavy to move. She ought to move away. Her long lashes blinked once, twice. It was too much of an effort to lift them again. She would rest, just for a minute.

When Robin woke, the afternoon sun was low in the sky. Pushing the Cathedral Mountain quilt away from her shoulders, Robin sat up and ran a hand through the masses of hair that tumbled across her face. She was now on the long couch and Nick was firmly ensconced in the chair. His regard was sober and steady. Robin rubbed her eyes, wondering how long he had been watching her.

"It's starting to snow again."

Robin sighed sympathetically. "I'm sorry. I don't think you'll be able to let your family know that you're all right for quite some time. This promises to be even worse than last winter."

Nick nodded, then asked gruffly. "Are you hungry?"

"Mmm. A little. Would you like me to fix you something?"

Nick eased his bulk out of the chair. "Actually, if you don't mind, I'd like to do the fixing myself. I need to do something. Why don't you stay there? You look too comfortable to move anyway."

Robin snuggled down into the warm quilt. "Mmm. Remind me to ask you over more often. I have a soft spot for any man who can cook. Now, if only you can do windows too."

"Fat chance," he mocked. "In this place you would need an army of men. What do you fancy?"

For a moment Robin was startled, then a deep color

stained her cheeks pink. "Oh, anything. Why don't you surprise me. That's half the fun of having someone else do the cooking."

Nick studied her thoughtfully with an arched brow until she colored even more. Robin slid down on the sofa and pulled the covers up around her chin. She pretended to be resting until she heard him leave the room.

CHAPTER NINE

Nick prowled the house looking for Robin. He had insisted on washing the supper dishes and had taken a quick
shower before trying to locate her. He was becoming a
little worried after he had checked the kitchen, garden,
dining room, and living room, all without success. This
house wasn't very big, and with windows all around one
would think that it would be hard not to see her. At last
he managed to locate her in the study. At the moment she
was kneeling, rummaging through a box of yarns.

"What are you looking for?"

Robin whirled around. The yarn tumbled around her
form so that she looked a little helpless tangled in the
colorful skeins. He already knew that it was a totally
erroneous impression. She had grit.

"Oh, you startled me. I didn't hear you coming."

Nick held up one long foot for her inspection. It was
covered with a thick sock.

"No shoes," he explained.

"Mmm. They were pretty much the worse for wear but
I put them under the bed."

113

"Guess I'll have to go back and look for them." Nick straightened, then changed his mind and walked over to Robin, who was still kneeling. He bent down and offered her a hand to help her up.

Robin came easily to her feet and then backed hastily away when she realized how overpoweringly close he actually was. She almost tripped over one of the skeins of yarn in her haste. Nick caught her gently in his arms and Robin froze, a new kind of wariness entering her eyes.

Nick released her and knelt before her, making himself appear smaller and thereby presenting less of an imposing threat. It was a trick he had often used with children and small animals who were uneasy with his physical bulk. He reached for the skeins and laughed. They looked like toys in his hands.

"What are you going to do with these?"

Robin indicated the weather outside. It was snowing more heavily than before. "It looks like you will be here for quite some time. I thought I would make you a shirt and a sweater." *Besides, it will give me something else to think about. You are much too charming for my own good, Mr. Saunders.*

Amused indulgence filled his eyes. "You make a lot of things, don't you?"

Robin ignored him and went back to sorting through the balls of yarn.

"Where are you going to make them?"

"In the dining room. The table in there is just the right size for what I need."

"Show me which of these bits and pieces you want and I'll carry them out for you."

"If you could carry the portable sewing machine, I can manage the rest."

Nick stood up, "Give in to me on this, Snow Queen. I've

114

been cooped up for so long that any physical activity is sheer bliss."

Robin took one look at his serious face and relinquished the bolt of midnight-blue fabric, her sewing box, and a half a dozen skeins of powder-blue yarn. "That's the lot. You can take it into the dining room. I'll be out in a couple of minutes."

She turned to a large filing cabinet and began rifling through one drawer. When Nick left the room Robin breathed a sigh of relief. That man was all man. Tall, strong, uncompromisingly male. He was also fascinating and possessed a captivating charm.

Her mind only partially engaged in the task at hand, Robin finally managed to locate the designs she had been looking for. A pirate shirt and a bulky V-necked, raglan-sleeve pullover sweater. Grinning broadly, Robin mused that her father wouldn't have been caught dead in either of them. But this stranger, Nick Saunders, seemed sure enough of his own masculinity that Robin was willing to bet that he wouldn't even bat an eye.

Nick stood with his back to the dining room table. The pristine whiteness of the snowy fields of the valley was magnificent. The fluffy snow that fell in a swirling mass from the black sky writhed and twisted in a seemingly endless dance of power and light. He had switched on the stereo in the corner of the front room and the music of Tchaikovsky's Nutcracker Suite filled the room. The music and the swirling snow were joined in a lighthearted, gay orchestration of movement and sound. They were the spirit of the season.

Nick listened absently to the clicking sound of Robin's sandals as she walked along the slate tiles of the hall and the dining room. Looking over one shoulder, he watched her extricate a tape measure from the sewing basket he had set on the dining room table.

Robin's words held a forced lightness. "I thought I would make the shirt first. Then you will have something else to change into when you get tired of the red wool. I can try patching up your jeans later, but I don't think they can be salvaged."

His two heavy palms rested on her dainty shoulders. "You don't have to do this," he said kindly.

Suddenly at ease in his presence, Robin laughed naturally for the first time. Dimples folded shyly in her cheeks. "Oh, yes, I do. For a couple of reasons. One, if I don't give you some other clothes to replace your torn ones, you may decide to roam around *au naturel* again."

"Again?" Nick eyed her skeptically.

"Well, you seem to have a penchant for appearing only partially clad whenever I see you. Look at you now."

Nick frowned. He was fully clothed.

"No shoes."

Grinning, he wiggled his toes under the thick woolen socks. "If my lack of modesty offends you, I could go scrabbling under the bed to try and locate where *you* hid them."

Robin ignored him. "Two, I have been dying to make this shirt design, but I need a model to try it on. No point in designing something if it can't be used. Besides, you have the build for it and my father doesn't. Much as I love him, the man has no shoulders. You have little else."

Nick had a self-conscious urge to stoop and hunch those very broad shoulders, but he could tell from the teasing glint in her eyes that she knew it, so he forced himself not to.

"Three, you can't always wear the red wool—you would be just like fresh fish—you'll start to smell."

"Like a brute."

"What?"

Nick raised the back of his hand to her nose. "I already do."

"Do what?" Robin was totally confused. He held his hand under her nose until its lightly scented aroma filled her nostrils. "Fabergé?"

"Brut," he confirmed.

She studied the teasing hulk in front of her. "So, it wasn't some kind of mental aberration yesterday? You always hold these inane conversations."

"No," Nick assured her solemnly. "It's quite a recent development. I never had a Snow Queen to tease before."

Robin reached for a pencil. Swiftly she wound her long brown hair into a figure eight and wove the pencil in and out of the strands at the back of her head. Then she began to tape his broad shoulders and long arms. Picking up another pencil, she jotted the measurements down on a thick pad of paper.

Nick eyed the pencil sticking out of the back of her head with wonder. The masses of waves bundled into a loose knot at the back of her head looked too precarious to last, but she moved with no effort or consideration for the improvised barrette.

"How in the hell do you do it?"

"Make clothes? It's not hard really. First you just—"

"No. Keep the pencil up."

"The pencil?" Robin began to laugh. "I don't know. It just works. I never question anything that works. I just accept it."

"Trusting little soul, aren't you?"

Color flooded her cheeks. Robin turned to spread the midnight-blue percale across the wooden table. Picking up the scissors, she cut a length of cloth from the bolt.

"Here, make yourself useful." She thrust the bolt into his arms.

117

"What do you want me to do with it?" Nick was amused by her studied air of nonchalance.

"Just smooth out any wrinkles and take it back into the workroom."

Nick laughed but did as she asked.

When he returned, Robin was cutting out pieces of the dark blue fabric. She used no patterns or pins, apparently following some kind of invisible guidelines.

"I have seen women sewing before, but not often. Unless my memory serves me wrong, don't you usually need some kind of tissue paper pattern?"

"Not me."

Nicholas laughed at the unconsciously proud statement. "What makes you so special?"

Robin shrugged, adopting his characteristic gesture without thinking. "It's what I do for a living."

Intercepting his perplexed glance, Robin elaborated. "I'm a designer. I make patterns. For a shirt like this I would normally make a muslin first, but under the circumstances I'll skip that step and go straight on to the finished product. It should be close enough for government work."

"What? Where on earth did you come up with an expression like that?"

Robin laughed. "I spent one semester working for a university professor. It was her favorite saying."

"What else can you make?"

"Just about anything out of fabric. I made the sweater I'm wearing and those quilts on the couch."

"Good heavens! Do you mean to tell me that you designed and made that quilt in the bedroom too."

Robin nodded, pleased with his reaction. It had been a mammoth undertaking and deserved all the recognition it received, although she didn't usually say much about it. Few people realized the amount of painstaking work it took to sew close to fifty-eight thousand half-inch pieces by hand, and then quilt around each one.

Nick, for his part, was speechless. He sat in silence watching her nimble fingers cut and shape the dark blue fabric. It seemed to be taking form before his eyes. At last Robin reached for a box of pins and began to shape the darts and gathers. She was totally immersed in what she was doing, totally unaware of any other presence in the room. Nick left the room quietly.

Wandering restlessly around the house, he found the design to be totally unique. The garden room fascinated him the most. It was truly a woodland scene inside the house. Having inspected the garden throughly, Nick headed back to the study. Apparently it doubled as a workroom and library as well. Nick searched through the books along the book-lined wall that backed the garage. He located a number of novels by James A. Michener and decided to reread *Centennial* because of its pertinence to his present environment. Taking the novel with him, Nick wandered back into the front room.

Robin was still absorbed in her sewing. The sewing machine whirred companionably in the background when Nick started to read the novel. Three chapters later he put it down. The book was as good on the second reading as the first, but he was aware of his muscles becoming cramped from his prolonged immobility. Looking up, he noticed that Robin had begun to hem portions of the shirt by hand. It didn't look like she had moved other than to trade in her sewing machine for a needle and thread. A hasty glance showed that she had been working on the shirt for about three and a half hours. Nick padded over to stand just behind her chair.

The heavy weight of his hands closing over her shoulders startled Robin. She jumped, stabbing herself with the sharp needle. A spot of blood welled from the finger. She stuck it in her mouth and mumbled grousingly.

A deep gravelly voice over her head rumbled. "You've been working on that for almost four hours. Aren't you tired?"

A long strand of cinnamon hair swirled in a negative response. Her finger still stuck in her mouth, she mumbled. "Nick Saunders, you scared me out of a year's growth!"

Nick frowned. "Who is Nick Saunders?"

Robin pulled her sore finger from her mouth. She sat gaping at the stranger.

Mirth twinkled in his eyes. His strong, steely fingers closed around her delicate wrist. Her hand was drawn to Nick's mouth. His mobile lips closed over the tip of her index finger. He suckled the blood away, never taking his laughing eyes from her startled ones.

Robin groaned out loud at the sensual feel of his teeth and tongue. She could not help her inadvertent response. Panting huskily, she asked tremulously, "Aren't you? You told me you were."

Nick stopped nibbling her finger. "When?"

"Last night." Sanity returned when his lips left her hand. She snatched it away.

His dark cobalt eyes deepened with a mixture of amusement and interest. It was reflected in his voice, although his words were perfunctory.

"No. I told you, I don't remember the last few days too well. But my name is Nicholas Armstrong."

"Are you sure?" Robin sounded doubtful.

Nick laughed. "Positive."

"Well." She sounded aggrieved. "Why would you tell me that you were Nick Saunders?"

Nick shrugged in a gesture that was becoming familiar to the watchful woman. "I don't know. Maybe I misunderstood. Maybe I was still dopey. Or maybe I didn't know then or couldn't remember. Is it important?"

Robin frowned, nibbling at her lower lip, sounding unsure. "I guess not."

"Look, my name is Nicholas Armstrong—Nick, for short. I am the only son of Maxwell Armstrong of Bloomington, McLean County, Illinois. I am thirty-six, unmarried, and run my own business, Armstrong Engineering and Computing Services, Inc. The company is located in Chicago and we have contracts from all over the United States and several other countries as well. I design tools and the computer equipment to operate them. I don't have my wallet with me, so I can't prove who I say I am, but there's a green Horizon in my garage that's registered to me, and a cleaning lady who comes in once a week who would be willing to vouch for me too."

"Is she registered to you too?" Robin mocked tongue-in-cheek, finally accepting his word for who he was.

"Nope." His tone was light and casual, but his dark eyes held hers firmly and there was a serious quality to his gaze. "I'm completely unattached and entanglement-free."

Robin hesitated for a moment, knowing that her response would set the stage for their behavior for the next few days. Why did she hesitate? What made her even think of engaging in a light flirtation with this man? He was handsome and virile, but then so were a lot of other men. Her lashes lowered to hide the confusion in her eyes. Still, it had been a long time since she had felt this attracted to a man. After Randy had died, she had started dating again, but it had always been casual, nothing intense, nothing involved. Would she be getting in over her head now? After all, he was a stranger . . . he wouldn't be staying . . .

With the conflict still unresolved in her head, she sent him a pert smile that didn't quite cover the indecision in her eyes. "Well, I do have my driver's license with me and my mode of transportation is a Jeep Wagoneer, but I'm afraid that I don't have a cleaning lady to come in and vouch for me." Her face took on a decidedly serious cast as she shook her head slowly from side to side while offering her explanation. "They don't do windows, you see."

Nick's laughter was deep and rich. "Mmm. I can't say that I don't sympathize. But . . ." Nick sat down in a nearby chair and drew Robin to her feet and then onto his knees. "How do I tell if you're heart whole and fancy free?"

Her brows arched in amusement at his direct approach. She had a feeling that if this man wanted something, he went after it—no holds barred. Was it apprehension that she felt . . . or anticipation? "I suppose you could just ask."

"Mmm. Maybe." His arms around her waist were warm and strong as they held her securely while his face loomed nearer. When his lips were only centimeters away, he paused, cocking one brow in a high, interrogative arch. "Well?"

"Well, what?" Robin laughed softly, knowing exactly what it was that he wanted to know, but deciding to make him work for her answers.

"Am I the first man to make your heart go pitter-pat?"

"No." She smiled. *Just the first since Randy.*

His brows lowered in a mock glower. "Mmm. A lady with a past . . ." Then his face cleared and he put on a decidedly hopeful expression. "Any chance that it was shady?"

"Nope, not a one," Robin replied smugly.

"Oh, well." Nick tried for a truly crestfallen look. "Not even paradise is perfect anymore." And Robin laughed too. "Any chance you're into lighthearted casual affairs?"

122

"Mmm." Robin copied his opening. "I have a feeling that those are more your style than mine." She smiled.

"No. Not really. At least not one-night stands." Nick couldn't even explain to himself why it was so important that he reassure her on that point, but it was. Then shrugging off the almost alien feeling, he started his bantering again. "Then I take it whatever involvement you've had has been of the most serious nature?"

"You could assume that." Robin smiled when he hesitated, and wondered what he would do next. She could almost see the wheels turning in his brain.

His cobalt gaze narrowing, Nick asked bluntly. "Are you married?"

"Not any more."

He waited. But Robin offered no further information. Very slowly his eyes lightened and the corners of his mouth tilted upward. "Ah-ha! A gay divorcee."

"Wrong again." Before Nick had time to comprehend the exact meaning of her statement, Robin lifted her arms around his neck and touched her mouth to his. Her lips were warm and red and laid like butterfly wings against his own.

Surprised, but not unwilling, Nick gathered her into his arms. One hand slipped to the ribbed waist of her angora sweater and insidiously eased itself under the fluffy material. His fingers kneaded the smooth, satiny skin at the small of her back. Then his long fingers played lightly against her waist before moving up to splay caressingly across her back.

Nick groaned as her delicate pink tongue darted across his lips. Her warm lips moved across his cheek and beard to nibble sharply at his ear. When her tiny, milk-white teeth sank delicately into his lobe, Nick removed his hand from under her sweater and ran his hands up and down her arms, kneading the supple flesh. When his fingers accidentally touched a bruise, Robin flinched, then shifted even more closely into his embrace.

Nick could feel the smooth muscles of her jean-clad legs against his own tensed, denim-clad thighs. He could feel her soft breasts brush against his chest through the fabric of their clothing. Desire rose in him. He wanted her so badly that he could actually taste it. But something wasn't right. He was as confused as she was full of contradictions. Earlier she had been adamant in her rejection, yet now she seemed pliant and perfectly willing. Why? What had changed?

Painfully his hands stilled their exploration of her flesh. Robin sat quiescent under his touch, content to be held by him. Nick was nowhere near as content. He had an almost unconquerable urge to pull her down onto the hard slate floor and make mad, passionate love to her until neither of them could move for the pleasurable exhaustion that would follow. He was not used to denying himself in this manner. Nor, for that matter, had any woman ever aroused him so quickly, so thoroughly, so completely.

"My God! Snow Queen!" His voice was harsh. "What are you trying to do to me?"

"My name is Robin." She wriggled, seeking a more comfortable position on his lap.

Nick groaned deep in his throat. "Robin. The harbinger of spring. Woman, what in hell are you up to?"

Robin sat up, dumbfounded. "I'm kissing you. What did you think I was doing?"

Stiffling a groaning laugh, he grabbed her hand and forced it down against the cramped muscles of his flat stomach. "Well, I'm sure as hell not just kissing you." he muttered sexily.

Robin didn't move her hand away from where he held it. She had been aware of his growing desire—after all, she had been married, but what she hadn't counted on was her own escalating involvement. She was attracted to him—who wouldn't be?—and she was willing to admit it. But all she'd had in mind had been a little lighthearted flirtation, nothing serious, nothing intense. Somewhere along the line she had gotten carried away by sensations that had been hidden deep inside her for years. Would he let her go? Or was she in too deep? Would there be an ugly scene when—

"Robin." His voice was incredibly soft as his strong arms crossed over her waist and stomach and sheltered her in the protective warmth of his chest. The lips that sought and found her nape set off a series of delicious tremors before they began to nibble a path to the lobe of her ear. His firm teeth sank in a painfully erotic love bite that lasted only a fraction of a second before his tongue probed the contours of her ear, leaving her a shivering mass of femininity. His voice was a silky purr as it stroked along her nerves to ignite a burning sensation in the pit of her stomach. Yet his voice was light—at variance with the mounting desire Robin was now intimately aware of.

"Why do I have this feeling that you're going to ask me to stop? You are, aren't you?"

Mutely Robin nodded her head.

Nick eased her away from him and stood, but with his hands still firm around her elbows he never truly relinquished her. His face was serious, his eyes still dark with mingled confusion and desire. "Why did you do it, Robin? You were so frightened earlier . . . why not now?"

Robin felt embarrassed, yet she met his eyes straight on, her expression as serious as his. "I never meant it to go so far. But you're an attractive man—a very attractive man —and, well, to be perfectly honest, I got carried away." Robin felt foolish admitting it, but she couldn't see any way out of it. It was the truth, and she had no doubt that he was aware of it anyway. After all, he had been the one to call a halt.

Releasing her elbows, Nick's fingers marked a slow trail down to her wrists, and then moved to capture and lift her hands to his chest. "How long have you and your husband been apart?"

Robin's chin lifted in unconscious, if somewhat belligerent pride, her eyes sparkling angrily. "I'm not sex-starved. A good roll in the hay won't cure what ails me. I just got carried away and it won't happen again."

"Ah. No. I didn't mean that. Truly." The dismay that he felt was evident in the tightening of his fingers and the sincerity of his tone. He drew a long, deep breath. "Hey, I'm sorry. I really didn't mean it the way it sounded, but now I don't know what to say without making it sound worse."

Robin's eyes didn't flicker for an instant. Nick's, however, did shift as he moved uncomfortably from one foot to the other. He hadn't felt this ill at ease since his mother had caught him misbehaving in the second grade. "Look" —his hand raked through his hair—"I thought maybe if you'd been hurt . . . Well . . ." He cleared his throat and tried again. "You can't see a lot of people up here. You said this place was isolated. And . . ." He took another furtive glance at her face and trailed to a halt. Amusement had taken the place of stony silence.

"We're not that isolated. And no, my husband didn't hurt me. We'd known each other since high school and we were were married during college. I loved Randy very much—perhaps even more than most young people, because we knew we had so little time." The humor left Robin's face, leaving her not sad, but sorry. "We knew when we got married that our time would be short. Randy was leukemic."

"Oh, God," he groaned. "Now I feel worse than ever."

He hadn't wanted to rake up painful memories, and while he wanted to offer his sympathy and the comfort of his arms he was afraid that she would see his offer as another bid to get her into bed. He didn't want to offer her that kind of transitory and fragmentary relationship. He didn't want that for her at all. Nick released her reluctantly. His arms felt empty without her. He had never felt exactly like this before, nor was it a pleasant feeling.

Robin eyed him questioningly, unsure of the meaning of the constantly changing expression on his face. "You've no need to. It was a long time ago. But—" Robin drew a deep breath and took the plunge. "I don't want to start something that I can't finish, and I don't want to finish what I started."

Nick's grin was as crooked as it was sympathetic. "Would you consider a fresh start?"

Robin cocked her head to one side. "What did you have in mind?"

Nick stepped back and pantomimed knocking on a door. "Excuse me, Mrs.—?"

"Lemery."

"Mrs. Lemery." He smiled gravely. "I seem to have inadvertently become stranded in the middle of a Colorado snowstorm. Could I impose on your goodwill and remain here for the duration of the storm?" Seeing the smile that was starting to spread across Robin's features, Nick continued with a twinkle in his own eyes. "I don't have enough cash with me to offer to pay for my room and board, but I'm a great hand with woodchopping and I can cook up a hearty meal with one hand tied behind my back. But . . ."

"I know." Robin's laugh was resigned, but her eyes sparkled with wit. "You don't do windows."

Nick shrugged without a trace of apology as his grin flashed white.

"Okay." She laughingly pulled him across the room toward the huge Christmas tree, and then sank down, Indian-fashion, on the thick pile of a sheepskin rug. "You can start here. It seems that I fell behind in opening my Christmas presents this year. You can open presents, can't you?"

"At thirty-six, I think I can claim to be a past master at the art of decortication."

"Hmpf." Robin gave a ladylike snort. "Twenty-dollar words don't impress me, Mr. Armstrong. You're not stripping the bark off a tree here, just gift-wrapping off a package."

The next half hour was spent companionably opening presents with Robin telling Nick about her mother's improving condition. Nick, for his part, revealed more of himself than he had done in years. Robin was a very good listener.

Suddenly Nick complained plaintively and loudly. "Hey! How come I get all the practical things like soap and shampoo and toothpaste?"

Robin feigned innocence. "Because those are the ones I bought and wrapped for myself."

"Cheat!" He grabbed for the one remaining box beside her.

"No!" Robin was laughing but the word was sharp.

Nick paused in removing the wrapping. "You know what it is?"

A blush suffused her cheeks, deepening them into a dusky shade of rose. "I think so."

"Well, well, well," he teased. "This calls for further investigation."

Her color spread, deepening into a fire-engine red as Nick removed the lid and whistled in startled surprise. His strong lean fingers lifted out the knee-length princess-cut

128

dress of white lace and jade silk. He handled it reverently. "On you, Snow Queen, this will be beautiful."

"Thank you." Her color was still high as she reached for the box.

"Wait, there's another one."

"No! Oh, please, Nick. Don't open it."

"Curiouser and curiouser. I take it you know what's in it?"

Robin nodded, unable to speak.

"Did you buy it?"

She shook her head. "No, my mother did."

Nick's smile was gently teasing. "I'm intrigued."

His hand gently pried the lid off—and froze. His fingers moved at a snail's pace, and inched downward to bury themselves in the pale yellow tissue. His large brown fist held a will-o'-the-wisp collection of feminine frippery. His fingers poked among the pieces, separating the four items. Gossamer-thin nylons laced with a silver thread glistened in the glow of the Christmas tree lights along with dainty bikini briefs and a delicate strapless brassiere of cobweb fine lace and dark jade-green bows. And the final item— tiny, exquisite, and very, very evocative—a matching garter belt.

His voice was filled with awe. "I have simply *got* to meet your mother."

129

CHAPTER TEN

The following days passed swiftly, as an easy camaraderie was established between them. The snow continued to fall intermitently and when the skies cleared the wind rose, blowing the snow into high peaks and sealing the valley off from the world.

Robin lay in her double bed watching the Stygian darkness turn into a misty gray and finally into a brilliant cerulean blue sky dotted with light fluffy cumulus clouds. The sun glinting off the snow-covered peaks was dazzling, filling the skies with a blinding white fire. Robin rolled over, burying her head in the pillows. For once she found no comfort in the shadowy hollow of the valley. Memories of the past several days flooded her mind.

They swirled and swooped round and round in her brain. It became almost impossible to separate and coordinate them. Robin sighed. It was not as though she had not been attracted to a man before. At the university she had been attracted to several of her classmates. While in college Robin could always find a date, even on fairly short notice. And then, Randy had stopped seeing her in the "kid-next-door" role.

Robin smiled softly. What she had felt for Randy had made everyone else pale in comparison. They had had good times and those were the ones she chose to remember. She would never forget him, and she never wanted to. Yet, the very nature of her relationship to Randy had only reinforced her selectivity. It was not as though she didn't enjoy male companionship. She did. But until this past week she had not found another man who could make her feel the way her husband had, and she had not been willing to settle for anything less.

Robin had never considered that her standards might be too high. When occasionally approached by this line in an attempt to obtain more of a response than she was willing to give, Robin had always been able to laugh lightly and say No, thanks, without any regrets. She knew what she was looking for. She wanted a permanent and satisfying relationship like the one her parents shared, and like the one she and Randy had shared so fleetingly.

Love—the kind of love she had to give—was whole and complete unto itself. It was the kind of love that had sustained her through the painful reality of Randy's illness. It was the kind of love that even six years later helped her to know her own mind.

Flopping over restlessly, Robin surveyed the bedding in disgusted amusement. It looked like a prairie dog town that had been in the path of a buffalo stampede. The covers were so tangled that she would have to strip the bed before it could be straightened. Robin grabbed her pillows and piled them up behind her back at the head of the bed. Knees drawn up to her chin, Robin stared unseeingly out of the window. Hunched as she was, her toes did not even reach halfway down the bed. Not at all, she reflected idly, like the gentle giant in her parents' room.

Now there, Robin admitted freely, *is the crux of the matter.* The Incredible Hulk that had shared her home during the past few days was exactly what she had been looking for as far as potential husband material was concerned. Unfortunately he did not appear to be looking for a wife—or if he was, he certainly wasn't looking in her direction.

Robin sighed softly. It wasn't every day that she found a six-foot-four-inch hunk of man lying around her living room. One would have thought with those kinds of odds in her favor that their fate would have been preordained. She couldn't understand it. Her still-scruffy guest was interested. She could see that. In fact, he was very interested. But since the evening when he had withdrawn from her caresses, he had made no attempt to do more than present her with a gentle peck on the cheek.

Oh, he teased and provoked her with clever, witty banter. Many of his utterances were filled with lightly teasing sexual innuendo, but he had made no attempt to advance his suit. His rambling during his illness had given Robin a disturbingly accurate picture of his normal outlook, and she could repeat chapter and verse on the number, place, and position of women in his life. Celibacy had not appeared to be his long suit, although he had not in any way come across as a philanderer. Sex was an important part of his life, an appetite of the senses that was to be fed when it rumbled and grumbled, like an empty stomach. But not to be gorged or overstuffed at every turn.

Robin knew that at first she had been admittedly relieved when Nick had not followed up his casual sexual baiting with actions. Later relief had become pique.

"I mean, really," she addressed the craggy peaks outside her home. "What woman wants to be ignored by a man with a proven track record like his? It's tantamount to being told that on a scale from one to ten you rate somewhere between a precocious twelve-year-old and an eighty-four-year-old grandmother."

Nick Armstrong was an intriguing man. A beautiful example of a virile male. Although the scruffy beard he insisted on keeping hid much of his face, it could not hide the gentle laugh lines around his eyes, nor the provoking grin that often appeared on his lips. That he was strong in the physical sense had never been in doubt; his sheer size and bulk had seen to that. His strength of character and his disturbingly amiable approach to life had been garnered and gleaned through hours of stimulating conversation.

Since Nick's arrival on the scene, Robin's lonely vigil had ended in more ways than one. Physically she was no longer alone in the house. Although she was cut off from her family by a distance of over one thousand miles and broken telephone lines, Robin did not feel lonely. Nick Armstrong had come into her life with a vengeance. When she had first seen him she had suspected that he could be dangerous—and she had been right. But the danger he presented was not a physical one. Instead, it lay in the emotional and mental spheres, for Robin knew that he could change and reshape her life into something totally unknown.

Robin punched the pillow behind her back viciously. *The trouble is that this situation is so . . . so up in the air. I don't even know my own mind anymore. One minute I'm thinking that any involvement, no matter how impermanent, would be worthwhile and the next I'm cursing myself for a fool. I can't live like that. I need to know where I stand. I need to know that the commitment would be two-sided. And yet . . . if it wasn't, could I love him any less?*

It was disgusting to care for a man like that, especially when the man in question obviously didn't reciprocate.

133

Hadn't the last few days shown that he could take her or leave her . . . and that leaving her was no hardship?

"Damn it! Damn it to hell." Robin swore softly, but with great passion.

Nick paused mid-stride. Perhaps now was not the best of times to be serving his charming hostess breakfast in bed. She appeared to be upset. For that matter, she had been as edgy as hell last night too.

Robin heard the rattle of teacups and turned to see Nick walk into her room.

"What do you want?" she snapped.

Nick blinked in surprise. No, now was certainly not the right time. Dark circles under her eyes and the rumpled state of the bedding indicated that if she had slept at all, it was only fitfully. He held out the tray and added in a pacifying tone, "I thought I would bring you breakfast in bed."

Robin had not been listening. Instead she had been looking. He wore only the tattered blue jeans that she had painstakingly managed to patch. His feet were bare as was his chest, covered with jet-black hair that ran from his throat to his navel and did not hide the muscles holding the tray. They rippled when he flexed his arms to push the tray into her line of vision.

Exasperated, she went on the attack. "Don't you like clothes?"

Nick lifted a thick brow in silent inquiry.

"Oh! Never mind!"

Nick put the tray down on a nearby chair. "Didn't you sleep well last night?"

"I slept fine!" She glared.

Skepticism was hastily wiped from his face when her glare increased in intensity.

"Just go away!"

Nick's spine stiffened. Temper sparkled from his cobalt

gaze. He hooked his thumbs in the loops of his low-slung jeans, and drawled silkily. "My, my, we are in a temper, aren't we?"

"Go to hell!" Robin turned her back, ignoring the warning signs that he was exhibiting. She slid back down under the twisted covers.

Nick's temper flared. The word he spoke was not one that a lady should hear. Robin pulled the pillow over her head. Amusement warred for dominance in Nick's face. Her gesture was that of a young child. Seeing a slowly fading greenish yellow bruise on her hunched shoulder, Nick decided to let his temper fade. She had had one hell of a week.

Devilry lurked around his lips, pulling his mouth into a sliding smile that cut deep grooves into his bearded cheeks. His rough hands quickly stripped the quilts and top sheet off the bed. Robin shot up in the bed, hastily reaching for the covers.

"What the hell! What do you think—Nick!" The last word was a shriek.

Nicholas scooped her struggling form up into his arms. "Stop squirming, Snow Queen."

"I don't squirm!" she flashed. "It's beneath my dignity."

A wicked grin slashed across his bearded features. "Your dignity is an iffy thing right now. Every time you move, your nightgown slips lower on the top and higher over your thighs. If you're not careful . . ." His brow arched suggestively just as his voice trailed to a goading halt.

Robin jackknifed into a stiff, unresponsive position; yet, her fingers clung to his broad shoulders, wanting the forbidden. She steeled herself to ignore the clamorings of her body and addressed him stonily. "Nicholas Armstrong,

135

put me down this instant. I'm not a child and I wasn't put here for your amusement. You can't just come barging—"

"Hey!" Nick lowered Robin to her feet. "*Pax!* Robin."

Without uttering another word, Robin turned with what dignity she could and found a housecoat. Pulling it determinedly over her arms, she ignored the movements of the tall man behind her. The less she concentrated on that bed, the better. For once she would be glad when spring came; cabin fever was really getting to her. It had to be that, it couldn't be—

"Your breakfast is getting cold." Nick's words interrupted her thoughts, shattering the solitude she had tried to impose on herself. Whirling around, she shot him an icy glare, while another part of her mind noticed that he had smoothed all the covers and turned down the bed.

"Robin"—he spoke softly—"I wasn't trying to annoy you."

She gave him an exasperated, disbelieving look.

Nick drew an *X* solemnly across his heart and then raised his right hand. When she glared at him, he grinned sheepishly. "Well, not at first anyway. Come on, Robin, eat your breakfast."

Mumbling a disgruntled pretext, Robin sat down and took the tray onto her lap. Halfway to lifting a piece of toast to her lips, she stopped and fixed Nick with a cool look. "You do have something better to do, don't you?"

"Than watch you? No." Nick sank down beside her on the bed. Grinning mischievously, he filched a piece of crisp brown toast.

Feeling her own lips tilting in response to his decidedly —and probably consciously cultivated—charm, Robin gave in to her desires and patted a spot closer to herself. "Make yourself to home," she encouraged with mock sarcasm.

"Thanks, I will." He scooted closer and slid his arm around her shoulders.

They sat side by side, munching companionably through the crisp smoky bacon, fluffy scrambled eggs, hot buttered toast, icy cold tomato juice, and thick, creamy hot chocolate.

"Do you want anything else?"

Robin laid her head on Nick's shoulder, enjoying the forbidden pleasure. What she wanted wasn't possible. She sniffed delicately at his musky male scent. It was lightly flavored with Brut. It teased her already-heightened senses. Forcing her mind to the matter at hand, she groaned. "Oooh, no. I couldn't eat another bite!"

"What you need is a tramp in the woods."

Robin burrowed closer. "No. It's too cold."

His large hand lifted the tray from her knees and,deposited it on the nightstand.

"A nice, long, refreshing tramp in the woods," Nick repeated teasingly.

Half in jest, half in earnest, Robin let her arms wind round his powerful neck and shoulders. Her breasts, through the thin fabric of her clothing, brushed his muscled chest. Suddenly Robin wasn't playing games anymore. Her breasts tautened, their peaks becoming outlined against the thin material of her peach-colored robe. She knew that Nick was aware of the changes in her body too.

Her breathing became restricted. A burning sensation started deep inside her, spreading its heat throughout her body. She shifted closer against Nick, letting him feel her mounting desire. All sense of proportion faded. Her legs moved seductively against his.

"No," she crooned. "It's too cold. Stay here and keep me warm, Nick."

Nick's blue eyes turned to flame. Robin's lips parted in anticipation of his searing kiss. Her cheeks prickled, already imagining the scratchy softness of his beard. The tip of her tongue appeared between her teeth. A slow, triumphant smile spread across her face, lighting her eyes. Robin felt Nick's fingers tighten involuntarily on her upper arms.

The next thing she knew she had been hauled across his knees, her face only inches from the chocolate-brown carpeting. One arm was caught securely behind her back; the other was searching wildly, trying to find a perch where she could steady herself as the fingers of Nick's free hand dug playfully into her ribs.

Robin scrambled wildly before finally succeeding in obtaining her freedom. Kneeling safely out of reach on the rumpled bed, she glared—or rather, tried to glare angrily —into his twinkling blue eyes.

"Brazen hussy! You are not going to keep me cooped up here any longer. I'm going for a walk and you have exactly ten minutes to decide whether or not you're coming with me." Nick rose from the bed and padded lightly out of the room.

The winds had finally dropped. Nick stood looking out the windows of the front room, his eyes searching the length of the valley. The peace and tranquility he had found here was undeniable. He knew that he would have liked to stay forever. In fact, there were a number of reasons why he would have liked to stay. And one of the most pressing was a five-foot-four-inch piece of femininity.

Nick grinned sardonically. It had been a close call. He had just barely made it out of her bed. If it weren't for the fact that he felt that this bizarre situation was half the problem, he would have been more than willing to reciprocate. In fact, the only reason he hesitated was that if he were to take advantage of her loneliness and she were to regret it later, he could never forgive himself.

Today she had seemed to want him as much as he

wanted her. And he did want her, desperately, and the small, self-satisfied smile that had spread slowly across her lips had been the only thing that saved her. Fortunately it had been annoyingly smug, like the cat with the canary, and had acted as a signal for him to stop. The trouble was that his bewitching Snow Queen could raise his blood pressure higher and faster than any other woman he had ever known.

Robin entered the room and saw that Nick had pulled on the powder-blue pullover she had finished a couple of days earlier. She felt that he must be thinking of his family. The two of them had spent a lot of time, during the past few days, talking. He was incredibly close to his friends and relatives. She felt as if she knew Nick's parents and Tom and Liz and their two children almost as well as she knew her own parents.

Nick had spoken at great lengths of his childhood. It had been very pleasant listening to his tales of adventure and woe. He seemed to have enjoyed college life and his work, but Robin detected a note in his voice that indicated that he no longer found Chicago to be completely congenial. Perhaps he might like to stay in or near this valley and the Rocky Mountains.

Looking at the mountains surrouding the valley, then looking at the man standing at the window, Robin acknowledged that for him she would willingly give up everything. He could be her life. Robin stood still for a few minutes, savoring the taste of selfless love.

"It looks like we can start digging out. I think the storms may have broken."

Disappointment flooded through Robin. She had almost forgotten that he had his own life back home. This was just an interlude. A night in the forest. There was nothing permanent about his arrival into her life.

"Yes. We should be able to take the snowmobiles into town tomor—"

The telephone pealed throughout the house loudly and stridently.

Nick and Robin stared at each other in dumbfounded amazement. Suddenly laughing, Robin launched herself into his arms, exclaiming needlessly.

"The telephone! Oh, Nick! The phone's working. Now you can call your parents!"

Nick lifted her under her arms, raising her high over his head and swung her round and round until they were both dizzy.

"Nick! Nick!" Robin cried breathlessly. "Put me down. If we don't answer it, they may hang up."

She ran for the extension in the study. "Hello?"

"Robin? This is Tim at the ranger's station. The telephone company's been working on our lines all morning, so I thought we would give you a call and see how you're doing."

"Oh, Tim, I'm so happy to hear your voice. I'm fine. I think the telephone men must have fixed our lines at the same time they fixed yours. This is the first time the telephone has worked since Christmas." She took a quick breath and continued. "I'm fine, really. Plenty of food and water, plenty of work. But I want to call my folks and the Marsdens down in Rifle and let them know I'm okay, so can I call you back later?"

Nick could hear the man's drawl. "Sure. I've some calls that really can't wait, anyway. We just wanted to make sure you were okay, otherwise if I couldn't raise you by phone, Sam and I would have come by snowmobile. Well, see you soon, Robin."

"Bye-bye, Tim. Give my love to Sam."

"Sure thing."

Robin hung up the telephone with excitement still sparkling in her eyes. Her cheeks were glowing, her lips parted and breathless. She was incredibly beautiful in an earthy, natural way. Nick felt a shaft of jealousy spear through his insides. Steeling himself against her undeniable charm, he made his voice cool, almost cold. "Who is Sam?"

Robin stared open-mouthed. Then began to laugh. "Sam is Tim's wife, Samantha. They're forest rangers up near Sheeps Head."

Nick was skeptical and angry. Apparently she wasn't as alone as she seemed to be. Then he cursed himself for an idiot. What did it matter if she wasn't alone? He was here with her now. It had been he she had invited to stay with her in her bed. Not some forest ranger.

"I believed you about Liz and Jill, so why won't you— oh, Nick!" She grabbed his hand and pulled him farther into the study. "Don't let's fight. You can call your father now and let him know that you're okay."

Nick capitulated after asking if she wanted to call her parents first.

"They can wait. Yours are more important right now. I just told Tim that because it was easier than trying to explain who you were and what you were doing here."

Nick pulled the phone eagerly toward him and began to dial. His hand hesitated over the last couple of digits. He hung up the receiver.

"I can't."

"Why on earth not?"

"My father has a heart condition, Robin. Suppose he's there all alone. Suppose the shock—"

"You dial, Nick, and I'll ask for Jill."

"Would you? I—I—"

Robin placed her fingers over his lips and handed him the base of the telephone. "Just shut up and dial, Nick. Everything will be fine."

The line rang four times before someone answered it.

Robin's knuckles were white with the strain. The man who answered sounded old and defeated, but the voice was so exactly like that of his son's that Robin knew she was talking with Maxwell Armstrong. Trying to suppress her inner excitement and sound casual and natural, like an old friend, she spoke quickly and lightly.

"Hi, Max! This is Robin. Is Jill around?"

She waited. "Could you ask her to come to the phone, please. I hate to interrupt her, but I can't call back later and it is long distance."

Robin turned to Nick, covering the receiver with one hand. "She's fixing lunch. I forgot about the time zones."

Nick pulled Robin onto his lap, holding her tight. "God! Robin, I'm scared."

"You're scared? I'm petrified! I know I'm going to— Hello? Hello, Jill?"

Suddenly Robin didn't know what to say. She cleared her throat a couple of times. "My name is Robin, Robin Lemery I live in Colorado. Jill, will you tell Max that Nicholas is all right. He's not even hurt. He's here with me now. I'll let you talk to him."

Maxwell Armstrong must have been watching Jill's face. The wires fairly roared. "Nick? Nick! Are you all right? Where are you, son?"

Robin held the receiver out to Nick. "I'm fine, Pop."

Robin tried to leave, thinking that Nick might like some privacy, but he refused to let her go. She buried her head in the hollow of his shoulder, breathing in his tangy masculine scent through the powder-blue pullover.

The conversation was long and protracted. Apparently Tom and Liz were there too. Much of the time was spent in explanation with every few sentences containing a repetition of assurances of good health on the part of Nick Armstrong. The conversation lasted well over two hours. Robin, still cuddled in Nick's arms, had begun to trace the deep V neckline of his sweater. The tips of her fingers were tickled lightly by the crisp jet hairs that covered his chest. She didn't realize that her actions were quite distracting.

"Tell them to go to hell, Pop!" Nick's voice was cheerful. Robin sat up in surprise. That was certainly a change from the yesses and nos she had been hearing for the past fifteen minutes. Nick gave her a reassuring squeeze.

"The woman I'm with has to call her family too. She wants to let them know that she's all right.

"No. She lives here, but the phones have been out since Christmas and she's here all alone. They're bound to be worried.

"No. I'm not going anywhere. Tomorrow will be soon enough to make all the necessary arrangements.

"I love you, too, Pop. 'Bye."

"What was that all about?" Robin asked doubtfully.

Nick grimaced. "Apparently the powers that be want me to stay off the telephone so that they can call at their convenience and let me know when someone can get here to pick me up and escort me home."

He added sardonically, "I gather it would offend them if I were just to go home on my own. They want to ask me some questions too. I said tomorrow was soon enough. Now, you had better call your folks and let them know you're all right. You had also better tell them about me. I would hate for them to hear about this over the news."

"Are you that newsworthy?" she teased.

"Hell! I hope not!"

Nick stood, lifting her high in his arms before depositing her tenderly back into the chair where he had been sitting. He knelt on one knee beside her, his eyes level with hers.

"I'll talk to them for you if you like."

A tiny frown pleated her brow. "Now, why would you want to do that?"

143

"They're bound to worry."

"It won't be so bad. Other people have gotten lost up here before, and we've been snowed in before too. I think once they know that everything's okay they'll be more excited by my mother's progress." Her hand reached out and squeezed his. "She may be walking now."

Catching her hand in his, he returned the pressure of her grip, feeling just a little sad that she could so easily turn her mind to other matters. It pointed out just how little effect he would have on her life.

"Well, then, call me if you need me." The last was addressed to the top of her cinnamon head as she bent to dial her parents.

Robin kept her head lowered. He would be going soon. There was no reason for him to stay. No reason at all.

"Hello?"

"Hi, Mom."

CHAPTER ELEVEN

This was the beginning of the end. Today was their last day together. Earlier the authorities had called and made arrangements for someone to pick Nick up and escort him to the airport in Denver. From there he would be able to catch a flight along with his "watchdog"—to use Nick's word—to Peoria. The last leg of his journey would be by car to his parents' home just outside of Bloomington.

Robin knew she was going to miss this man who had appeared on her living room couch and disrupted her life only ten days earlier. He had become the most important thing in her life. She would have liked to have begged him to stay on, or even to have pleaded to go with him, but Nick would undoubtedly want to return to his own sane and sensible life-style. He would want to forget everything and everyone connected with his ordeal.

A snowball caught Robin soundly on the shoulder, rocking her almost off her feet. Robin took shelter behind a hardy Colorado blue spruce and returned the attack with vigor and accuracy until Nick adopted a different tactic and marched toward her, ignoring her volley of snowballs. When he was about twenty feet away, Robin fled, but she did not get more than five paces away before Nick tackled her and tumbled her into the snow, his heavy weight practically burying her in a high drift.

A chinook had raised the temperature about twenty degrees above normal and it felt like early spring. When Robin grabbed for one last handful of snow, Nick pinioned her hands and held them securely manacled over her head.

"Insolent minx!"

"You started it!"

"I'll finish it too!" He laughed and grabbed the half-formed snowball from her fingers.

"No! Oh! *No!*" Robin wriggled, pushing his body away with her knees.

"I'll rain icicles down on your head!" she threatened.

"Will you now, Snow Queen? I think I'll have to take preventive measures."

"How?" Insolent provocation was in her voice.

"By melting your ice." His large hand laid back the material of her coat, exposing her nutmeg-brown pullover and slacks. The hot-pink blouse underneath the pullover was no pinker than Robin's cheeks. Nick's head blotted out the sky.

Somewhere along the line, the kiss changed. Nick fumbled with the zipper of his parka. His gloves and a rising tide of desire made it impossible to open. He tugged off the glove on his right hand with his teeth and finally managed to open his outsize parka before lowering his body to the exquisite welcome of hers.

Robin moaned and arched her body to his. When Nick loosened his grip on her wrists, she ran her hands down his chest to his waist, where they clung tightly. She felt his warm, consuming mouth eroding her senses. He kissed her, each time a little more deeply. The fingers of his hand

146

slipped beneath her sweater, tugging her blouse out of her slacks, and then ran lightly across her back.

Robin pulled away, breathless. "Oh, Nick! Your hands are cold!"

"So warm me." He growled a laugh into her throat. His warm, loving lips grazed a devouring path from her throat along her jaw to end at her shell-like ear. Then back again. He drank thirstily at her kiss-swollen mouth.

When Robin arched herself against him in total, mindless abandonment, Nick whispered wickedly, "See. I told you I would melt the icicles."

Robin gasped. "You conceited hulk!"

Laughing, she struggled to be released. Nick held her effortlessly. It was heady, thrilling, exciting, lying deep in the snow, surrounded by his warmth. However, Robin soon perceived that resistance would not get her revenge; so she resorted to enchanting feminine wiles.

"I can't breathe," she moaned plaintively.

Equally cunning, Nick stated seriously, "I'll breathe for you."

His strong fingers pinched her nose, while his warm moist lips pressed her mouth open. His rough-bearded cheeks brushed against hers, and the sweetly scented air from his lungs filled hers. Shocked by his sensuality, Robin lay savoring the sensation of having him breathe for her. Mouth to mouth resuscitation had never felt like that before.

"Now, you breathe for me." Nick commanded, rolling over onto his back and dragging Robin on top of him.

He gasped, groaning deep in his throat when one shapely knee slipped between his powerful thighs.

"Oh, God, Robin!" He pulled her tight, scorching her very soul with his overpowering kiss. His fingers probed her scalp, sending ripples of pure pleasure down her spine. He kissed her eyes and nose and cheeks, trailing hot moist bites along her jaw from ear to ear. Yearningly he pulled her more fully onto him, until both of her legs slipped between his.

Robin became intimately aware of the hardening masculinity beneath her soft body. Her breath caught in her throat. An answering pulsation of burning desire started in the pit of her stomach. But Robin forced herself to remember her role, and the importance of revenge.

She braced her forearms against his chest and lifted her head away from his seeking lips. The thick mane of her cinnamon hair parted naturally at her nape and cascaded down either side of their faces, hiding them from all but their own eyes.

"Behave yourself and I'll breathe for you, Nicholas."

He groaned, but leisurely slipped his hands down to knead the muscles at the small of her back. "I'm being as good as I can."

Robin laughed, moving off his bulk, and knelt in the snow by his head. She pinched his nose and covered his mouth with her own. His tongue searched for hers. Robin choked and spluttered.

"Nicholas! Behave! Or I won't breathe for you!"

Again Nick groaned, but he forced his hands to remain tightly clenched at his sides. His voice was hoarse and husky. "All right."

Robin smiled and lowered her head. Once. Twice. Her hand slipped under his sweater and across his diaphragm, lingering on his chest. Nick groaned again.

"Shh. Don't talk. Just relax," she coaxed him.

Twice more Robin breathed sweet life into him, then her hand slipped into the snow, gathering a huge handful. One last breath and she slipped her snow-filled hand across his burning flesh.

Nick jerked upright like a man who had been shot,

frantically trying to pull the snow from under his bulky sweater. "What the hell—"

"That's just a rain of icicles!"

"Why you—"

Robin turned and fled, her open coat flapping in the winter air. When she reached the house she flew through the dining room.

Nick caught her and pulled her down at the edge of the short flight of stairs that led to the front room. Robin clung to the wrought-iron stair rail.

"Safe! Home!" she shrilled.

Nick ignored her cries and hauled her onto his knees, but Robin was taking no chances. She quickly turned around to wrap her arms tightly about his neck and pressed her body to his, whispering audaciously in his ear. "Play fair, Nick." Her eyes were sparkling and full of laughter, inviting him to join her. "Don't make me tell your stepmomma that you don't honor the rules of fair play."

Unable to resist the laughter in her, Nick stood, tumbling her down the last step and onto the floor of the front room.

"Minx!"

Robin laughed up at him from her sprawling position at his feet. "What else could I do? I couldn't let you melt all my ice."

"Snow Queen," he warned her with a throaty growl.

Robin scrambled to her feet and ran lightly to the other end of the house. "I'm going to wash my hair."

Forty-five minutes later Robin sat in front of the fireplace. A colorful terry-cloth towel was draped around her bare shoulders. She had changed into a strapless dress. The bodice was shirred and clung tightly from breast to waist, where the skirt flared fully over her curving hips and thighs to end in a silky swirl just above her knees. Her bare legs were curled underneath her as she carefully combed the tangles out of her still-damp hair that was almost black when wet.

Nick came into the front room with a large glass of orange juice, and eyed the spring-green dress happily. An outfit like that didn't leave much to the imagination. It covered all it was supposed to—and even some more besides—but it didn't take a college degree to imagine what was still hidden.

"What's for supper?"

Robin eyed his tall figure askance. "Cornish game hens. Do you eat all the time?"

A grin slashed Nick's bearded features as he defended himself. "It's the mountain air."

Robin eyed him disdainfully as she mocked. "Sure it is."

Kneeling down beside her, Nick took the comb from her fingers and handed her the orange juice. He began combing the waist-length strands. "It smells like the mountains."

"That's the well water." Robin took a sip of the drink.

Nick continued to comb her hair even after it was dry. Robin relaxed under his ministrations, enjoying the feel of his hands and the closeness of his body. Nick dropped the comb and threaded his fingers through her hair, spreading its silk like a fan across her bare back and shoulders. "Do you always dry it like this?"

Robin shook her head. Long cinnamon strands tumbled and twirled around her back and shoulders. "In the summer I sit in the sun."

She took another sip of his orange juice.

"Hey! That's mine."

"Oh," she teased. "I thought you were giving it to me for the privilege of combing my hair."

"Privilege?" Nick scoffed. "It was work—and hard work at that."

Nick filched the glass from her hand and placed it on the tile near the fieldstone fireplace. Kneeling over her, he brought his face close to hers. Robin hastily pulled back. Nick advanced his attack. "It's too late, Robin. This is one scrimmage I intend to win. One little kiss won't hurt you, now, will it?"

Robin's arms encircled his neck. "No," she encouraged him softly. "One little kiss won't hurt."

As kisses go, it wasn't so little, but it sure didn't hurt.

Nick dried the last pan as Robin rinsed out the sink. He laughed softly, knowing that he could get a rise out of her.

"Are you going to Clorox the dishrag tonight?"

"Cloth." Robin responded absently, but automatically. "No one would want to wash dishes with a rag."

When Robin leaned down to reach under the sink for the Clorox, Nick placed his hands on either side of her, trapping her between his arms. Robin stiffened slightly.

Nick backed off in surprise. "What's wrong, Robin?"

She ignored him, putting the dishcloth to soak.

"It's really incredible, you know." His voice sounded overawed with wonder. Robin looked up, puzzled, thinking that she had missed some of the conversation.

"What?" she asked blankly.

"How long you can take to put a rag to soak."

Robin flushed and started to turn away, halting when she felt a sharp tug against her scalp. Turning with him so close had tangled her long hair with the buttons on the cuff of his shirt, trapping her.

Noticing her predicament, Nick teased softly. "I'm glad I changed my shirt before dinner. Now I have you where I want you."

"Would you untangle me, please?"

"You will have to pay a forfeit."

Robin looked up quickly, then down again when her hair pulled. Trying to inject a light note in her voice, she laughed, saying that in that case she would do it herself.

Nick let her struggle on alone for a few minutes before he finally captured her hands.

"Here. Let me. You're making an even worse mess of it."

It took a long time to remove the silken strands from the buttons at the cuff of his midnight-blue pirate shirt. For some reason his own fingers had grown clumsy. By the time he was finished she was trembling.

Robin backed hastily away, unsure of his seriousness in claiming forfeit. Suddenly she did not want Nick to touch her. He was leaving tomorrow and she did not like it, not one little bit.

"Running away, Snow Queen?"

"No." Her voice showed a trace of brittleness. "It's just that I—I have a lot of work to do."

"I have a lot of work to do too," Nick added suggestively.

Robin left the room hurriedly.

Nick followed her into the front room. "Why don't you want to be with me tonight?"

"It's not that—I guess I'm just edgy because I'll be alone here after tomorrow."

"You could come with me to the airport."

"No. I have too much work to do," she answered, picking up her sewing.

Nick sighed and turned to the stereo. He flicked through a pile of records, choosing several of the most romantic. Their lyrics and melodies filled the air.

Robin echoed Nick's sigh. That man could wrap her around his little finger if he but knew it. Sighing again, Robin stared unseeingly out into space.

His strong fingers prized open her hand, removing needle and thread and fabric. Nick pulled her into his arms. Robin's resistance was only token. This was where she wanted to be anyway.

"What do you think you are doing?"

"Dancing."

"Maybe I don't want to dance with—"

"Well, I do. So just shut up and enjoy it."

Robin stiffened when John Denver's "Annie's Song" began to play.

Nick pulled her tightly back into his embrace. "Look, Robin. I want to make love to you so bad that I hurt. But I know you're scared and I know that it wouldn't be fair to you. If you dance with me, I'll be able to hold you and touch you and enjoy you in my arms, but it won't get out of hand, okay?"

Hesitantly Robin relaxed in his arms, letting the music and lyrics flow over her. She wasn't scared—not of him.

Nick gathered her closer, letting one hand rest at the small of her back, rubbing it gently while the other slid up to her bare shoulder blades in order to press her into his chest. Robin felt her own arms sliding upward to encircle his neck. Her fingers toyed with his jet-black hair. She burrowed her face into the side of his neck, brushing a kiss along the corded muscles when she felt his hand slide across her shoulder to finger her nape. His fingers were strong as they threaded through her hair at the base of her scalp, pushing her head closer into his neck.

They danced for nearly an hour, Nick's hand moving lightly up and down her spine all the time, making Robin a quivering mass of nerves and desire. The longing continued even when his hands ceased their tormenting movement and rested firmly around her waist. The brushing movements of his powerful thighs against her softer, more rounded legs began to have a soporific effect.

153

They had stopped dancing now, their only movement being the swaying of their hips. Robin was practically asleep on her feet, warm, content, and drowsy in his hold. She lowered one hand from its position around his neck and traced the deep slash of the pirate shirt she had made for him. It had turned out even better than she had expected. His broad shoulders filled it admirably. It was open almost to the waist, where it tied with a single knot. Robin walked her fingers delicately up the expanse of his chest. The palm of her hand rested lightly over his heart. The beat was solid and reassuring.

"Happy?"

"Mmm." Robin snuggled closer, letting her lips part and the tip of her tongue explore the hollow at his breastbone.

"Robin. Look at me."

Robin lifted her drowsy, shadowed jade eyes to meet with burning cobalt ones. She offered no resistance to his kiss, allowing his warm lips to mold and shape hers. When his tongue penetrated her inner sweetness, Robin moaned like a sleepy cat deep in her throat. Her fingers buried in the crisp black hair over his heart, kneading with the reflex action of a dainty kitten. Nick could feel her contentment.

"Robin, you're driving me crazy."

Her slender arm moved upward to join its mate around his neck. Her body arched arousingly against his. "Good. You make me feel the same way."

Nick lifted her high in his arms, and carried her swiftly down the hall to her bedroom. His lips never left her. He laid her gently on the bed, then reached down to tenderly remove her arms from his neck. "I can't stay, Robin. As much as I want to, I can't."

Robin's fingers went to the tie of his close-fitting shirt, expertly undoing it. She sat up and leaned forward, trailing hot, fevered kisses across his chest. "You have to stay, Nick. I need you."

"What you need is a spanking."

She looked at him sadly. "Nick, don't tease me now. I'm serious. I'm hurting."

"God, Robin. I hurt too." He gathered her into his arms and stripped the covers back from the bed, lowering her once more to its cushiony softness.

Robin lay quietly for the moment, watching his heavily breathing form. He was so handsome—and so necessary for her happiness. Sitting up, Robin's dainty fingers moved to slip the pearly buttons from his cuffs and eased the shirt off his broad shoulders. "Lay down beside me. I want to be with you."

Flesh burning with desire, arms aching for the feel of her supple body, Nick began to rain kisses across her face and neck and shoulders. Reverently his hands cupped the mound of her breast through the bodice of her dress. A hard little peak of desire sprang to life under his knowing touch.

Robin shivered uncontrollably as Nick's strong hand moved to knead her hip. His mouth nibbled its way down the column of her throat to the scented valley between her breasts. His teeth caught at the fabric of her bodice and tugged with a sensuous intent until her breasts were bared to his sight.

His hand at her hip slipped lower down the smooth length of her thigh only to reach under her skirt and move unerringly up the satiny flesh of her leg. Supple, stroking fingers teased their way across her bikini briefs, kneading intoxicatingly along the bones of her hip.

His lips lowered to tease the rosy peak of her breast. He nibbled lightly until Robin felt she was suffocating from her desire. She moaned and writhed sensuously beneath him, arching her back in invitation. Nick's tongue traced

155

the lowest curve of her breast where it joined her rib cage. Robin's fingers kneaded frantically at Nick's shoulders as she sighed longingly. Her hands moved to his head, guiding it to her throbbing breasts. She gasped with unheralded pleasure when his tongue licked and flicked the ripe peaks, igniting a fire of mounting passion deep in her womb. His hands, wonderful, glorious hands, moved across her flat stomach and caressed her navel until her brain and lips were crying for fulfillment.

"Oh, Nick. Love me."

"I want to," he groaned huskily as he kissed her jawline. "You have no idea how badly I want to."

The fingers of her small hand fluttered daringly across the dark fabric of his jeans. "I know," she urged softly. "I know."

Nick lowered his forehead to her breast, not to stroke or arouse her, but rather to gain control of himself, but Robin forestalled him by threading her fingers through his thick, dark hair. She had never seemed more beautiful to him than she did when she lifted his head so that his eyes looked directly into hers.

"If you won't make love to me, then I'll have to make love to you." The dark jade of her eyes told him just how serious she was as her fingers traced across his bared shoulders and down the brawny length of his arms to brush lightly across his fingers.

When he made no move toward her, Robin sat up, knees tucked to one side, and reached for the hem of her dress. Gathering it carefully in her hands, she pulled it over her head in one graceful movement. Yet she could not release the fabric immediately, fearing that Nick would reject her. Instead, she used the yard of cloth to shield herself from his gaze. For any other woman the gesture would have seemed coy, but with Robin, Nick knew instinctively that this time she did not mean to tease,

156

but rather, that the gesture was almost self-defensive, showing him clearly that she was not perfectly sure of her ability to make him desire her completely. Slowly her eyes lowered; her free hand reached up to draw her long hair forward to cover herself.

Such a simple gesture, yet for him—he could not turn away. Unable to resist, Nick's hands sought hers and removed the pale green fabric from her grasp. Robin sat very still, her hands resting lightly in her lap, making no attempt to cover herself as he traced the curving slope of one breast through the strands of her hair. She was so beautiful, so trusting.

Robin was scared, not that Nick would continue, but rather that he would not. She needed him tonight and needed him in a way that went beyond just the physical world. When his strong hands stroked her throat gently, easing his fingers around her neck and then lacing them through the hair at the back of her head, Robin hardly dared to breathe, knowing that this was Nick's moment of truth. If he withdrew now . . .

"Be sure, Robin." So soft, so tender. "Be very sure."

Robin raised her face, her eyes shimmering with love and a hint of relief. He cared. "I'm sure," she whispered.

The hands at the back of her head separated and drew her hair back off her shoulders and breasts. "You are so beautiful, so very beautiful." His words were thick with desire. While one hand drew her hair down the length of her back, smoothing the strands tenderly, the other hand lifted slowly to trace the arch of her brow, the length of her nose, the width of her lips, and the line of her jaw. "You're so very tiny, so very fragile. I'm almost afraid to touch you for fear you'll break."

In answer, Robin's fingers moved to the snap on his jeans. She was exhilarated when he drew a sharp breath as her fingers brushed against the flat muscles of his hard stomach. Made bolder still by the sudden tightening of his grip on her shoulders, Robin dared to lower the zipper, then hesitated before touching him briefly with wondering fingers.

But Nick was no longer capable of holding back. Gently he eased her onto her back, spreading her long hair out across the sheets. His eyes glittered cobalt fire as they traced the beauty of her breasts and the supple grace of her limbs. Robin could feel her nipples tightening under the intensity of his stare. When he stood she knew from the fire in his eyes and the gentle, caressing touch of his fingers that his absence would be only momentary. He would not leave her tonight.

Sighing softly, she watched him strip his clothing from his body in one smooth move. However, she had only a moment's fleeting glimpse of his body before he joined her again.

His hands were gentle as he eased her remaining garment from her. And then those same hands were infinitely more gentle as they skimmed her breasts and stomach and thighs. His lips were everywhere, telling her of his desire. "Robin," he whispered, "I want to be one with you. To hold you in my arms, to feel you around me, to touch you and make you mine. I——"

Robin caught his face in her hands and drew him down to her, kissing him deeply. She loved the feel of his beard against the palms of her hands and the springy texture of the hairs of his chest as they brushed against her breasts, making her tingle with untold pleasure. She had never felt like this before and for all his strength and power, he touched her with gentleness and consideration, somehow knowing instinctively that there had been no one since her husband.

Her heart and mind bursting with love, she followed his lead without hesitation. Touching, stroking, caressing, loving, and when his hair-roughened legs moved to settle between her silken ones, he found her eager to give herself up to the glory of his desire.

He came to her slowly, tempering his burning need with a control born of pure love, and she enfolded him with an eagerness that took his breath away. Then they were one and love swamped each of them so intensely that even breathing seemed difficult.

"Okay?" he asked tenderly, and was answered with her passion-drugged kiss and a gentle stroke of her quivering hand.

"It's beautiful," she sighed softly. "More beautiful than anything I've ever known."

His throaty groan told her that there was more to come, and experienced woman though she was, she could not envision any glory beyond what she had already experienced in his arms. But then when Nick continued to touch her and kiss her and teach her love's true meaning with strong, powerful strokes of fulfillment, Robin found herself moaning soft sighs of encouragement and delight. She clung to the one familiar being who filled her life with a newly discovered world of sweet sensation and passionate expectation.

She felt on fire. A burning sensation grew within her and filled every vein, every pore. Her breath came in quick, shallow gasps as her body learned to scale the glorious heights of love and desire. As Nick swept them both higher and higher into passion's majestic splendor, pressure built inside Robin, cutting off her breath and searing her with its heat. Then she was suddenly free, floating in the arms of her lover, bound only by the tethers of his powerful embrace. His weight was heavy, surrounding her, holding her, protecting her. And he—her man, her mate—was the only security she needed in life. As long as he was with her she would never come to harm.

He would teach her to climb the mountains and soar the heights far greater than any of those she had previously known. She had grown and matured over the years and the love she had to give reflected it.

It was several minutes later before Robin became consciously aware of Nick's strong hands stroking the damp tendrils of her hair away from her face. Had he lain watching her? Did he know her thoughts? Had she pleased him as he had pleased her? A slow-rising blush covered her cheeks; yet she snuggled trustingly in his arms, smiling up at him. "I feel like I have this huge, silly grin on my face."

His soft words of love told her that their union had been as special for him as it had been for her and Robin's pleasure increased a hundredfold. Trustingly she raised her lips to his for a slow, deep, tender kiss. The kind of kiss that only lovers share.

The time they shared together just touching was a quiet time, a time of deep peace and utter contentment. Their hands made languid, half-forgotten forays that were not meant to arouse but rather to remind each other of the beautiful moments of oneness they had exchanged. A feathering of fingers, a brush of lips, a softly spoken word, yet it was enough.

But reality could not be forever held at bay. Robin sighed softly. How ironic that when she once again found the one man to whom she could give her heart, it had to be a man who was not free to stay. He was her lover for all time. For her, there would be no other. She had made her commitment and though he had no knowledge of it, her commitment was for a lifetime. Yet he was leaving her tomorrow. She had wanted him, needed him, loved him. But she knew that she did not have the right to demand that he stay with her, or that he take her with him. Could he really leave her after the tender loving they had shared?

When Robin's hand brushed across Nick's chest, he

caught it and drew it up to his mouth, pressing his lips into her palm. His blue eyes were dark and troubled as they met hers. "I hope it was as beautiful for you as it was for me, Robin."

Robin knew what he was saying, and knew that it was something that she did not want to face—not yet. But there was no escape and it would have been unfair to leave him wallowing in remorse. Her hand turned to cup his bearded cheek; her thumb traced his full lower lip.

"I have no regrets, Nick, I can promise you that." *No regrets that it happened. I only regret that it must end.*

He kissed her then with a passion that had her clinging mindlessly within seconds. When he released her, she lay panting in his embrace. Age-old conventions set aside, she asked softly, pleadingly, "Do you have to go?"

His anguish was great. He did not want to leave her, not now, not ever. But he really did not know what else to do. She needed time. She was so alone. He knew what loneliness could do. Hadn't he taken lovers to dispel the ache? The two weeks that they had shared were too unrealistic, too isolated, too intense. Suppose that in the future she came to regret her impulsive actions. "Yes." It was an agonized groan. "I don't want to go, but I must. For both our sakes. We need time to decide if this is real or only desire."

Robin's eyelids lowered to hide her grief. She had to recognize the truth of his statement, not for herself, for her commitment had been made for a lifetime. She had known that she ran the risk of being left alone, but she loved him so. It really did not matter whether tonight was only a dream or a promise for tomorrow. Her love for Nicholas would not change. She loved him deeply, without limitations, and without bounds. The tears that clogged her throat were not easy to suppress, but suppress them she must, not for her own sake, but for his.

I'd go with you for as long as you liked, be it a day or an hour or a century. I have so much love to give you. Why can't you feel the same? "No regrets, Nicholas. Either way. What we have is very precious to me." She kissed his lips lightly. "I have enjoyed sharing a night in the forest with you."

Nick breathed deeply as his hands moved to smooth the bedcovers up over her satiny flesh, flesh that had risen to his bidding. "Robin, I'll be honest. If you weren't so important to me, I'd do as you ask." *Do what I want,* he thought to himself. "But I care too much to use you. I couldn't bear it if you were to regret it later."

Robin wound her arms around Nick's neck. "I love you, Mr. Armstrong. I would never regret it."

Nick's bearded face nuzzled her neck. "If only I was as sure."

"Nick?" Her voice showed her surprise. Did he regret it? Was he sorry that they had shared such sweet desire? Her lips parted, ready to ask him, but Nick forestalled her, placing his fingers over her mouth. "Shh, Robin. No more words now. Just turn over and go to sleep. I find I can't leave you after all." He turned her in his arms and pulled her into the shelter of his body. What she had felt for Randy had been a young girl's love that might have grown with time; what she felt now was a woman's love—more mature, better defined. Robin closed her eyes.

Late into the night Nick's lips brushed against her hair. "Not tonight," he whispered softly. "I can't leave you tonight. Dear God, Robin, how I love you. How I wish I could keep you for my own."

Nick was still awake when dawn crept over the towering mountains. The sky glowed red and gold from the shafts of sunlight that rained down from the sky, bathing the land in a rich, golden light. Nick felt the tension building within himself. He was not looking forward to

162

going home, although he desperately wanted to see his family and friends.

Robin lay quietly in his arms. Her breathing was light, but Nick suspected that she had been awake for quite some time. He had lain next to her all night, not sleeping, but holding her in his arms.

"Robin."

It was the first time he had moved in almost an hour. She had thought him to be asleep. "Mmm?"

"Come with me."

Her heart leaped in her breast.

"To the airport."

Disappointment slowed its beat. "Why is it so important to you?"

Nick's hands ran lightly over her body. He cupped her chin, tipping her head back against his shoulder. "How can you ask me that this morning?"

"But nothing happened."

"Didn't it, Robin?"

Her eyelids fluttered shut as a light blush rose to her cheeks. Yes, something had happened last night. She had given her heart away and given it so completely that she would never be whole again unless Nick was beside her. Yet she loved him enough to want what was best for him . . . even if it meant sacrificing herself. She could not hold him. He had to be free to go. Yet, even so, it was not just a one-sided relationship, for in a way, she, too, had found freedom. Or rather, a taste of freedom, for to her, freedom was possible and fulfilling only when she was within the boundaries of his arms and the warm shelter of his body.

His firm mouth gently brushed against her forehead. "Robin, I realize that making love is not something that you could enter into lightly. I know you're not the kind of woman who would want a relationship that wouldn't last. You are very special to me—very special. But I don't

163

know if what we have is enough." *I could never give you up if you were to change your mind,* he reasoned to himself. *It's better that I give you time now, better if we both have time to think, both have time to be sure.* Nick rolled onto his side and pulled her close to his chest. "Robin, I want to be with you as long as possible." His kiss was long and deep, but passionless. "And I'm scared."

"Scared? You?" Robin was astonished. "Of what?"

He shrugged. It was a gesture that had become heartrendingly dear. "Of a thousand things. Of having to go back. Of seeing my friends and family . . ." *But mainly, of never seeing you again.*

"Don't you want to see them?"

"Yes, of course I do."

Robin was thoroughly confused.

"I just feel so unsettled inside. Being here has been . . . This place is so peaceful. I don't want to leave it." *I don't want to leave you.* "I'm scared to go out and face the rat race again. Yet I know I can't stay. I have commitments to myself and others. My family, my friends, my business.

"I had hoped you would come with me—to the airport —because I wanted to stay close to you and to what this valley means to me for as long as possible."

Robin sighed. She did not want to see him off, especially not now when his leaving her would mean that she would be hurting a thousand times more than she had when she lost Randy. And because she knew she would break down and make a fool of herself at the airport. The thought of never seeing Nick again was killing her. Yet how could she refuse his request. She desperately wanted to spend every possible second with him. Any stolen moment of time with him was worth all the sorrow that their parting would bring.

"All right," she capitulated.

Nick buried his face in the strands of cinnamon silk, his hands stroking her back lightly as he murmured, "Thank you."

Robin wanted to turn to him, to bind him to her physically, emotionally, and morally, but she realized that it would not be fair to him. In his own way he was hurting every bit as badly as she was. Nor did she feel that she could make the offer again. Last night had been a magic madness of moment and intent. Today, in the cold light of day, no, she could not make that offer again.

"They will be here soon. I suppose we should get ready."

"Yes." Nick seemed particularly loath to release her. His lips rested lightly on her forehead. "I will miss you, Snow Queen."

"I'm only a phone call away," Robin suggested hesitantly. Why did it take courage to say those words? No man could make love like he did unless—

"No."

So flat. Could she have heard him correctly? Did he want no contact? She had known that he would want to forget the kidnapping, but could he forget her so easily? For a moment she wanted to beg, but she could not. She had gone on after Randy died. This, too, she would survive.

"Robin." He caught her hand and drew it to his lips. He wanted to explain, but how could he? It was so hopeless. She was a part of this place and could not leave. And he? He had a duty to family, friends, and employees. Nothing had changed. Making love had only made their parting that much harder. Meaningless telephone conversations over long-distance wires would only make him ache to have her in his arms. Why couldn't he stay? Why did he have to be torn between duty and longing? Why? Why? Why? His fingers tightened around hers until she gave a little gasp of pain and brought him back to the present. "I'm sorry, Robin," he whispered huskily. "Calling you, talking to you, would only prolong the agony. We both need time to think."

She had known men could desire without loving, but she had not thought that Nick would do that to her. Still, he had never lied to her. He had been open and honest and the love she had—still had—for him had been freely given. There would be no recriminations on her part; she would not cling. She would give him no cause for sorrow.

"It's all right, Nick. I understand, and I agree. To continue something that neither one of us is in a position to finish would be cruel and painful for both of us. I'll miss you too." Robin raised her face for his last kiss. It was gentle, an expression of mutual regret. Nick drew her closer and deepened the kiss. It changed to a slow, sensual demand. Robin placed her hands on his shoulders, kneading their taut muscles lovingly. When the kiss threatened to grow out of hand, Robin withdrew gently. "I won't be ready if I don't get dressed now."

The airport lobby was crowded. People rushed back and forth between the counters, the luggage area, and the doors leading to the airplanes. Men and women kissed their families good-bye with tears and sorrow, but it was not the same type of despair Robin felt. These people knew that their loved ones would be returning. All Robin knew was that this man had come into her life, filled her senses with his presence, and now he was leaving. Their interlude —their night in the forest—had been fleeting. And now it was at an end. She would never see him again.

Robin sat quietly in the lobby. Her fingers intertwined with the steely grip of the tall man at her side. Neither noticed the pressure of the other's grip. Each was locked in their private thoughts of grief at their impending separation.

Nick studied the woman beside him, smiling tenderly at the picture she made in her turtleneck sweater, jeans, and brown boots. She looked very much a part of this country —pure and natural. Nick sighed, knowing that it would not be fair to make any decision at this point in his life— not if it were to harm her. Everything was in too much of a turmoil. Leaving her was like leaving a part of himself. Yet leave her he must.

"Mr. Armstrong." The agent's voice broke into his intense concentration. "They have just called our flight."

Nick stood, drawing Robin into his arms. Neither seemed to know what to do or say under the circumstances. He traced the line of her jaw with an index finger. "Take care of yourself, Snow Queen. I'll miss you and your Rocky Mountain valley."

Robin smiled wanly.

Nick's finger curled under her chin, lifting it. He kissed her lips lightly. "Mostly though—I'll miss you."

For the first time, Robin realized how absolutely final a good-bye could be. She could not just let him walk away. She needed to feel his arms around her once more. Her fingers caught at the open front panels of the parka Nick had shrugged into. Pulling him closer, she rose on tiptoe. Her arms slid up his chest and wrapped themselves around his neck. Her fingers lost themselves in the luxurious texture of his crisp blue-black hair. Her soft body pressed against his harder length. Tears sprang to her eyes and clung like sparkling drops of dew on her thick lashes. Her lips crushed against his in a brief moment of regret and passion. "Be safe, my heart."

Nick groaned, gathering her body to his. His voice was shaking, his words deep and pain-filled. "Oh, Robin, why in hell did this have to happen to us. It's too late now. I have to go . . ."

Robin pressed her soft mouth against his, stopping his words. Nick assumed command of the embrace; his arms crushed her to him until Robin felt her ribs would break. His mouth ground down on hers, his tongue parted her lips and teeth, ruthlessly seeking to draw her soul from her body. Robin could feel one muscular hand as it slid under the wool of her sweater, spreading across her shoulders and spine. His other hand gripped a handful of her cinnamon hair and held her face to him. Robin's flesh burned from his touch. Her eyes smarted from suppressed tears and her throat ached and burned. She could feel the dampness that sprang to Nick's body, increasing his already potent, enticing masculine scent. It filled her senses.

It was a kiss that made many of the airport-goers—seasoned travelers used to passionate good-byes—uncomfortable. This kiss was different. More intense. More painful. This man and woman were not saying good-bye for a day or a week or a year—but forever. An eternity of being alone. Most of the people turned away, leaving the tragic couple to what little privacy could be afforded them in the crowded terminal.

One man did not. He was an amatuer photographer who realized that the emotion was so painfully intense that it would prevail throughout any medium. He reached for his 35mm camera. He meant no harm. No intrusion. It was just that the intensity of their passion drew him. Something outside himself compelled him to preserve their parting for all time. Its pathos was timeless.

Robin wrenched her lips from Nick's, burying her face in the hairy side of his jaw and neck. "Nick, you have to go now."

"God, Robin! How can I leave you?"

Her eyes were sad as she brushed her palms over his

168

sideburns. "How can you stay? You have other commitments."

Nick looked as though he would like to argue. His hands clenched tightly, then turned her in his arms and pushed her toward one of the embarrassed agents.

"Take good care of her." Nick's words were gruff.

The man, who had a daughter of his own, gathered the slender woman into his arms. "I'll take her home, Mr. Armstrong."

One last time Nick allowed his hand to stroke the length of her silken hair. He turned abruptly and strode quickly away—not looking back.

Robin turned within the agent's loose embrace, removing her head from its hiding place in his shoulder. She watched Nick until he disappeared from sight.

"I guess we had better go now." Her voice was husky with tears.

Patrick Murphy lead her to his car and helped her into the front seat. Her face was turned away from him when he entered the car. Her small hands were fumbling with the clasp on her shoulder bag. They were shaking so badly that she could not manage the simple catch. He handed her a large, white handkerchief.

"Thank you." Robin began to cry.

Patrick started the car and drove away.

The night in the forest had died at the new day's dawn.

CHAPTER TWELVE

Once again Jill and Liz were seated around the kitchen table of the Armstrong farmhouse in Bloomington. Both pairs of eyes were filled with concern, their voices tempered with worry.

"Liz, he isn't acting at all like himself."

"I know. We were told that he might be reluctant to talk about it, but this—this is something different."

"Exactly." Jill pushed a cup of coffee at her stepson's friend. "I can't put my finger on it though."

Liz nodded thoughtfully. "It's as though he's a million miles away. All of a sudden you're talking to him and he doesn't hear a word you say."

"Do you suppose he was hurt?" Jill answered her own question. "No, you're right. It isn't like that. Something catches his attention and suddenly he's someplace else."

Max and Tom entered the kitchen, drawn by the smell of roast leg of lamb.

"Who is someplace else?"

Jill grimaced. "Nick."

Max sighed regretfully and shook his head slowly.

"Where is Nick anyway?" Liz asked.

"Max and I left him in the study. He went off into another of those blue funks of his. He's staring into the fire right now."

Liz added worriedly, "I know he was upset and moody before Christmas. I just thought he needed to get away from it all. But since he's been back he's worse than ever. I'm not saying spending a week or so isolated in the mountains was exactly what I had in mind when I said he needed to get away from it all—but I never thought it would make him so—"

The telephone interrupted her, and Max answered it. "Hello? Oh, hello, Mavis. Did you want to talk to Jill?" Max asked. He handed the receiver to Jill, who tucked it under one ear and raised her eyebrows in mute apology to the others in the kitchen.

"Hello, Mavis. What can I do for you?"

The remainder of the one-sided conversation was brief. "No. Yes. Really? Okay. I'll have to check, but I'm sure we do. Okay. Thanks for calling, Mavis. Bye-bye."

"What was that all about?" asked her husband.

Jill frowned. "Mavis said there was a picture of Nick in one of the newsmagazines."

Tom shrugged. "What's the big deal about that? He's been in and out of those for years."

Jill continued to rummage through a pile of reading materials, sorting through them until she found the right issue. "Mavis said something about a photography contest."

"When did Nick take up photography?" Max asked.

Jill thumbed through the magazine until she found the article. Skimming it quickly, she explained to the others. "Apparently they ran a contest for human interest photographs and the pictures in this issue are the contest winners." She turned the page. "Oh!"

"Honey, what is it?"

Silently Jill laid the magazine down, spreading open its colorful pages. The full-page color photo was so lifelike that the central figures in it appeared to be alive and breathing. The background was muted and out of focus. The central figures alone were in clear, sharp detail. The young couple were locked in a passionate embrace. Their emotions were so strong, so raw and passionate, that the viewer could feel them and shared in their grief.

A bearded, hairy Nicholas—almost unrecognizable in an outsize, torn, and ragged parka—was holding the slim body of a brown-haired woman in his arms. The woman's arms were wrapped around his neck, her body partially hidden in the loose folds of his coat.

The expressions on the couple's faces were riveting. Nick's was filled with desire and longing, the woman's with despair and the sweet sorrow of parting. And love. Total and complete commitment. Her commitment had been caught by the camera as well as the pain in her eyes. It was not a joyous photograph. In fact, it was painful to look at the picture for too long a period of time. The raw emotions reached out and touched every person in the room.

Jill smoothed the page. "It's called 'Love's Last Good-Bye.' The photographer took it in Denver just after the New Year. It says here that he didn't know who the couple was, but that everyone in the airport could tell that they were desperately in love and being forced to part. James Hunter, that's the photographer's name, said that he just had to capture their poignancy. It was so final."

"Final," Liz whispered. "It's tearing me apart just to look at it."

Jill turned to Max. "What should we do?"

"Show it to Nick." Max was decisive.

"Show me what, Pop?" Nick moved lithely into the

kitchen. The players in the scenario jerked like puppets on a string. Jill hastily tried to cover the picture.

"What are you hiding there?" He plucked the magazine from behind her and started flipping idly thorugh the pages, looking for what had captured their interest.

His hands froze. Color drained from his face. *Robin! There was Robin! In his arms!* He was feeling it again—the awful wrench of parting. The awful empty nights that followed days that were no more than aching voids without her.

He looked up. "I tried to tell myself that it was just the bizarre circumstances. The peace and tranquility of the valley. A thousand things. I knew it wouldn't be fair to her—or to myself. I couldn't stay; she couldn't leave. But it isn't any good. I have to go back."

Max rested a heavy hand on his son's shoulder. "When will you leave?"

"As soon as I can pack a few things."

"When will you be back?"

"I won't be back, Liz," Nick said solemnly. "I couldn't ask her to leave her mountains. They're too much a part of her." His voice was dreamy. "A rain of fire in the sky. I've seen that too." Then more firmly, "I could never ask her to leave and, to be frank, I don't think I could leave it again either."

"But what about the company?"

"You and Tom can take it over. You can run it together. I'll help with any designs you need. Just have the lawyers draw up a transfer of title and send it to me to sign."

Tom and Liz began to argue forcefully, but Nick was adamant. Max added his voice to the melee.

"Hold it!!" Jill's shrill two-fingered whistle broke the air. Her eyes were excited. "Look, I know this is going to sound crazy but, well, hear me out first, okay?

"Now," she continued briskly. "The way I see it Nick is determined not to come back. Right?"

"Right!"

"And you want Tom and Liz to take over the business, but they don't want to because you built it up, right?"

"It's more than that," Tom explained. "It just wouldn't work without Nick. I can manage my end fine and Liz is all set with hers too. But only because we are a team. Alone we couldn't survive. We need one another."

"So you want to keep on working with Nick?"

"Definitely," the Jenkinses chorused.

Jill hugged her husband. "I feel positively pioneerish. Okay, now for our end of it. I have been after Max to sell the farm and get a smaller place, where he could take it easy. At sixty-two Max isn't old, but I don't want him taking stupid chances with his health either. We were going to tell you tonight. We decided to put the farm up for sale."

She turned to face the Jenkinses. "And I know both of your parents have talked about moving somewhere closer to Chicago so that they can see the kids more often, right?"

Liz and Tom nodded in confused agreement.

"What is all this leading up to, Jill?" Nick asked impatiently.

"Pioneer spirit, Nick. Good old-fashioned pioneering. Why not move the company to Colorado. It's only fifteen people including Tom and Liz. Anyone who wanted to move could come with you and keep their jobs. Anyone who didn't or couldn't could have his or her position filled by someone in Colorado. And I'm sure the ones who stayed behind wouldn't have any trouble finding work. Your company has a terrific reputation. In fact I'm sure that if you called Riley's or S.A. & T. they would snap them up."

Turning to the Jenkinses, she added excitedly, "I'm pretty sure your folks would be willing to move too. I know Bette and Mayme and John have all told me that it was only Chicago—and the big city atmosphere—that put them off moving closer before.

Liz was incredulous. "You mean for us all to go?"

"A wagon train!" Max laughed, not knowing why the idea was not as shocking as it should have been.

"Yes!"

"No." Nick's voice was flat.

No one said anything until Jill asked tentatively. "Why not?"

"I can't wait for the move. I have to go now."

"We could handle most of it by ourselves," Tom offered. "It's not as if we would have trouble moving. We are still a fairly small concern."

"I would still have to spend weeks away from Robin. And there are other problems too." He paused. "I don't know if she will marry me. If she says no, I'm going to have my hands full concentrating on changing her mind. I won't be of much use to the firm."

"You could at least think about it," Tom urged.

"I'm sorry, but no."

Jill snatched the magazine from Nick and waved it under his nose. "Nick, you're creating problems that just don't exist. Look at her. *Look at her face!* That woman would follow you to the end of the world and not even know that she had left the mountains. Nick, I know that look. It was mine when I thought your dad was going to refuse my proposal."

Momentarily diverted, Nick laughed in astonishment. "You proposed to Pop?"

Jill defended herself, blushing. "Well, he had this stupid idea that he was too old for me."

She reverted back to the matter at hand. "In fact, I

wouldn't be surprised if your Robin proposed to you the minute she sees you." Jill was firm.

Nick's expression softened tenderly. A lean brown finger traced the bright hair of the woman in the photograph. "I think she did," he murmured. "I think my Snow Queen already did."

The woman who answered the door was petite and slender. She leaned heavily on a cane. She was Robin in thirty years' time.

"You must be Nicholas Armstrong. I recognized you from Robin's description. Won't you come in?"

"Thank you." His eyes searched the house for Robin.

"Robin isn't here right now."

A faint flush entered his lean cheeks.

"Please," Margaret Peters urged. "I would like for you to meet my husband. He's in the study right now."

Nick nodded, following her slow gait.

"Lewis, I'd like you to meet Nicholas Armstrong."

The older man eyed Nick with a faint hostility that became more pronounced as the inspection continued.

"What do you want?" he asked ungraciously.

Nick ignored Margaret's reproving "Lewis!"

"To marry Robin," he stated blandly.

"What makes you think I'll let you?"

"It's not your decision. It's Robin's."

"What makes you think she wants you? You've been gone a long time. Maybe Babe's found someone else."

Nick blanched, remembering the rangers, then called to mind the photograph and the last kiss they had shared and the days of growing to care . . . and their night of loving. "I'll take my chances."

"You left her once. You might do it again. I don't think I want Babe seeing you."

Slow anger burned in Nick, but he hung on to his

temper although his words were coldly contemptuous. "When I first came here I was hurt, my mind fuddled. I had trouble separating reality from fantasy. Would you be more pleased with me as a prospective son-in-law if I had taken your daughter away with me without even giving either of us a chance to decide if it was love that we felt for each other or only propinquity?"

"What makes you think she'd have gone with you?" Lewis asked sarcastically.

Nick eyed the tall, narrow-shouldered man in front of him antagonistically. He straightened himself proudly, stating coldly, "What makes you think she wouldn't?" Then with baiting anger, "What makes you think she won't?"

Lewis eyed the angry young man thoughtfully. He was certainly determined. *But then so am I.* No one was going to be allowed to hurt his daughter the way this man had and get away with it when he calmly showed up again. "Chicago is no good for a girl like Babe. It would stifle her."

Icicles dripped from Nick's mouth. "I'm not taking her to Chicago."

Margaret broke in softly. "Where would you be taking her?"

Nick scanned her face for hostility and found none. She was remarkably like Robin in appearance. "I'll be staying here in Colorado. I would never ask her to leave here. I know what it means to her. My company will be moving out here. In fact, we had thought to ask your husband to design our new plant."

"I don't take bribes, young man!"

Nick's temper got the better of him. He was seething. "It's not a bribe. I don't need you or your permission for anything. The only thing I need is Robin. And whether or not I get her is Robin's choice. Not yours."

"I don't like you, Mr. Armstrong."

"Then you had damn well better hide it when Robin is around. It will only make her life hell to have her father at odds with her husband."

"You're awfully sure of Robin, aren't you?" Lewis mocked nastily.

"No." Nick eyed him coldly. "Just sure of myself. Robin will have to make her own choice, but it would be better if she wasn't aware of your hostility."

"Better for whom?" Lewis goaded.

"Better for Robin. She's the only one who counts," Nick snapped.

"Just so you know."

At the end of his patience Nick snapped again. "Know what?"

"That Robin is the only one who counts," Lewis replied blandly.

Suddenly Nick's temper was replaced by wry humor. If he were in their place, he would feel exactly the same. "Mr. and Mrs. Peters, Robin is the only one who *ever* counted. If it had been only for myself, I would have married her before I left. The only reason she is still your daughter and not my wife is because I thought she deserved better than to be rushed and coerced into a decision she might come to regret. My only mistake was in being too cautious. It wasn't until I saw a photograph of us that I realized that what I felt, Robin felt too."

Seeing no change of expression on Robin's father's face, Nick added roughly, possessively, "Where is she?"

Lewis leaned back in his chair and put his feet up on the wide wooden desk. A twinkle appeared in his eyes when he saw his wife's amused face. A slight smile tugged at his lips. "You know, Maggie, I think I might have been wrong. I may decide to like him after all—in thirty years time."

"He sounds just like you when you approached my father."

Lewis ignored the angry young man in front of him and shook his head, pursing his lips before taunting his wife. "Ump-unh. I think he's got it worse."

Lewis deftly ducked to avoid a plump cushion that was hurled his way. "Well, Mr. Nicholas Armstrong of Armstrong Engineering and Computing Services, Incorporated, my daughter is down by the lake at the edge of the forest."

Nick turned stiffly to leave, only to be halted by the softer voice of Robin's mother. "Be good to her, Nicholas. She deserves the best."

Nick turned back. "You won't object?"

"Neither I nor my husband will object if you truly love Robin."

Simple. Plain. Unequivocable. "I do."

He turned and left the house.

"I like him, Lewis."

"So do I, Maggie. Much more than I expected. But Robin is so besotted with him that she won't even think of herself. It won't hurt him to have to stay on his toes for a while."

"You think he'll smother her?"

Lewis looked thoughtful. "No," he said slowly. "No. If anything, I think he'll give her whatever she wants."

"And she wants him."

"Mmm. Maggie? I do like him. Just don't tell him so for a while. He'll figure it out soon enough for himself."

Nick spotted Robin immediately. The weather was unseasonably warm, even for early August. She lay on her stomach wearing a pair of faded blue jeans and the same angora top she had worn at Christmas. She was drawing a sketch of a tiny mountain fern. The tip of her tongue was

179

clenched between her teeth. She was singing softly to herself. It was "Annie's Song."

Suddenly she flung down her pencil and pad and began to cry. Nick continued speaking the words. Lovingly. Seriously.

She stiffened at his first words, whirling to stare at him, hardly daring to believe her eyes. She had almost given up hope.

"Oh, Robin." His voice broke. "Let me love you again." He held out his arms.

Robin flew to his arms. He held her so close that her ribs almost cracked with the pressure. Nick rained kisses over her eyes and cheeks and nose. Robin melted into him, wrapping her arms around his neck and twining her fingers into his crisp jet-black hair. She pulled his mouth down to hers. Her lips parted to the thrusting, thirsting presence of his tongue. Hungry for his touch, Robin returned his caresses kiss for kiss, touch for touch.

Nick knelt and pulled Robin down to lay on the ground. The grass tickled her shoulders as it poked through the angora of her sweater. She felt it because her senses were so heightened, but she did not notice it because she was attuned only to the man in her arms.

Her arms still wrapped tightly around Nick, she pulled him down on top of her. He drank from her lips like a man who had been without water for days, months, years. Robin moved underneath him, inviting him to deepen his touch. Suddenly lighthearted and knowing that everything would be all right, Nick muffled a laugh along her throat.

"Don't tempt me, Robin. I don't think your father likes me as it is."

"Daddy?" Robin lay back panting. "When did you meet my father?"

"About ten minutes ago."

"Why wouldn't my father like you?"

"Because I'm going to take his daughter away, aren't I, Robin?"

She melted into his arms, pulling his mouth to hers, running her fingers through his hair. "You know it."

Her fingers began to toy with the buttons on his shirt. She began to laugh. Nick rolled off her and propped his head up with one hand. The other rested lightly across her waist, brushing rhythmically across her smooth stomach and occasionally making darting forays down to her hips.

"What's so funny, Snow Queen?"

"You. Me. Today."

"That's what I always liked about you, Robin. A nice, calm, sensible attitude. Always answering my questions with complete details. What about me and you and today?"

"Well." She rolled onto her side and began to unfasten the buttons on his shirt. When Nick tried to stop her she slapped his hands away. "Behave yourself."

"I am—*you're* the one who is undressing me." His fingers gripped hers, holding them fast against his heart. "Stop it, Robin. I'm serious."

Laughing, she desisted. "It's just that when I first met you I thought you didn't like to wear clothes. You never seemed to have too many on at any one time. Today you're wearing much too much."

"Witch." Nick leaned forward to kiss her nose.

Robin pushed him back and searched his face.

"What's wrong, Robin?"

"You look different. I've never seen you without your beard."

"Do you mind?"

A teasing light entered her eyes. "I don't know. Kiss me again and I'll let you know."

181

It was quite some time later before Robin pronounced that she liked him either way.

"Are you sure?"

"Yes. Kiss me again and I'll show you."

Nick's head ducked low, his teeth closed over the taut peaks of her pulsing breasts through the angora fluff. "I always said you were a hussy."

Robin slid lower into his arms, meeting his mouth with hers. "Only with you, Nick. Only with you."

"When will you marry me? I don't think I can last another minute to make you my wife."

"Hmm," she drawled laughingly, "if you had a special license, I'd marry you today."

"Well, then, you had better change. I've got the license burning a hole in my jacket pocket."

Robin lay back startled. "Really? You're not just teasing me?"

"I picked it up this morning."

"Oh, Nick, give me an hour and I'll be ready to go with you anywhere."

"Robin. It won't always be easy. I'll have to be gone a lot the first year or so."

"Gone? But you—now that you're here I hate to let you go again."

"I was going to give up the business, but Tom and Liz as well as Jill and Pop talked me into trying to keep it. I just couldn't let them all down."

Robin frowned. "Why would you give it up? I thought you liked inventing."

"Because I wanted to be with you—all the time."

"Well, Mr. Armstrong." Robin snuggled closer into his arms. "I hate to sound mercenary, but how would we eat if you gave up your business?"

"Oh, I would have found something else to do—but Jill suggested that I move the business here and Tom and Liz both preferred that, too, so I'll have to spend a good deal of time in Chicago tying up loose ends."

"Can't I go with you?" Robin asked plaintively.

"Would you want to leave here?" Nick was surprised.

"Nick." Robin eyed him solemnly. "Don't you understand? I love these mountains more than anything in the world—except you. You are my mountain, my valley, my life."

"It won't be for long, Robin. I promise."

"Then you will take me?" She sounded thrilled at the prospect.

Nick began to laugh. His hands moved suggestively over her body. "After a suitably lengthy honeymoon."

Robin slid beneath him with a slow sensuality that took his breath away. "Oh, God, Robin. Have I told you how much I love you?"

Her fingers traced the springy mat that ran from his belted slacks to spread across his pectoral muscles. When Robin's fingers brushed tauntingly across his nipples, Nick's breath caught sharply, then just as he began to think that he might breathe again, Robin's tongue began to trace the hollow at the base of his throat.

"Has anybody ever told you that you talk too much, Mr. Armstrong?" Her fingers smoothed his shirt off before they moved to daringly catch at the intricate buckle of his belt.

Nick muffled a low laugh along the side of her sweetly scented neck, taking in the mingled odors of her perfume and the summer grasses as he helped her ease off the rest of his clothing. When he moved to help her free herself of her clothes, Robin pushed his hands away, wanting to keep him in suspense, wanting to fill him with the same burning, aching need that filled her. She kissed and teased every part of his body with her warm, moist lips and her graceful, fluttering fingertips. But each time he reached for

183

her she pushed his hands away until at last he lay in tight control, knowing that only when she was ready would she succumb.

The feel of her denim jeans and soft sweater were torture to his taut body, for Robin had refused to remove anything but her sandals, yet Nick held himself from capturing her and forcing her to submit to his superior strength because he could understand what she was doing . . . even if it was unnecessary. After he had lain with her and loved her so, there had been no thoughts of other women in his mind and in his heart. The joy she had given him had erased all other memories. They were both starting fresh, starting anew . . . and he would allow her whatever license she needed to be certain that he would remain hers forever.

Robin's tongue was quick to trace the line of his lips. She was burning with desire, yet she meant to stall for as long as possible, knowing that Nick, for the moment at least, was inclined to humor her. Each time she kissed him it was a little deeper. Each time she stroked him it was a little longer, a little stronger.

"Do you want me, Nicholas?" she whispered throatily, tenderly moving his thick, black hair off his brow.

"I love you, Robin."

She trailed a line of moist, provocative kisses down his neck and chest, and then, daringly, to his navel. "Yes." Her tongue teased him both verbally and physically. "But do you want me?"

Nick groaned, knowing that she would not give in until he pleaded, but as much as he wanted her, he was loath to take the pleasure of her game from her. At this moment in time he understood her better than she understood herself. She needed to know her power over him was complete. She needed to know that no one could take her place.

"You'll never know how much," he moaned softly.

"Oh, I don't know." She laughed softly in return as the fingers of one delicate hand brushed knowingly against his abdomen and lower, leaving him almost breathless. He had not expected her to be so bold, but he should have known better. She was as wild and free and untamed as her mountains. Nothing would tame her spirit.

His fingers caught her wrist, pulling her hand away. "I want you, sweet witch. I want you with every fiber of my being, with every breath I draw, with every beat of my heart."

Robin laughed. It was a joyous, carefree sound and he knew that she would not keep him waiting much longer.

With one lithe twist of her body she rose to stand beside him, slowly divesting herself of her clothing. She could see the fire that burned in his cobalt eyes and knew that an answering fire was growing from deep inside herself. She loved him so! As he watched she stepped out of both her jeans and panties in one graceful movement. Her fingers reached for the hem of her angora sweater, hesitating briefly. She laughed down at him. "This is my favorite sweater." She drew it up over her head as she sank to her knees beside him and drew the sweater across his chest, abrading his sensitized nipples. She bent low, kissing his mouth with a lingering softness. "The sweater feels just like your chest does when we're making love."

Nick could wait no longer. With a lithe twist of his rippling muscles he pushed her back against the soft grass and her hair spilled out around her lovely face and smooth shoulders. Her hands were firmly anchored over her head, making her seem small and helpless within his grip; but it was a helplessness that she reveled in, knowing that his love for her was as great as hers for him. When the springy hair of his chest abraded her already-taut nipples she gave

185

a moan of sheer ecstasy as she arched her hips in supplication and invitation.

Nicholas met her mounting desire with an unleashed passion and power that left her senses reeling and drove all coherent thoughts from her mind. Never before had she experienced such beauty, such togetherness, such oneness with man and nature.

The spiraling pleasure that she had thought beyond compare grew and grew as Nick used his hands to stroke her tenderly and his husky voice issued words of love that urged her higher and higher. Then, suddenly, as his arms tightened around her and his loving words lost themselves in the softness of her flesh, she was soaring, flying free over mountains and valleys that seemed to pale to insignificance in comparison to the powerful protection and the tender tranquility of her lover's arms. When Nick's body, too, dissolved into exquisite shudders of release, Robin knew that their oneness was complete and that their future would be filled with a lifetime of forevers. And that knowledge shone from her jade eyes and was transmitted to Nick through her delicate fingers that feathered his body with love and understanding.

Lifting himself reluctantly away from her, he was hesitant to see the expression on her face. He had not been gentle. He had wanted her far too badly and his desire had flamed out of control. "Robin?" The word was low, husky, and filled with concern.

"Oh, Nick," she sighed, wrapping her arms tightly around his neck, threading her fingers through his black hair and glorying in the heavy, hard warmth of his body hovering just inches over hers. "I don't think I'll ever get tired of this, do you?"

His answer was a low, soft laugh. Easing himself onto his side, he cradled her tenderly while his hand stroked her gently from her shoulder to her thigh.

Robin lay content in his arms, barely taking in the sounds of the lake's water as it lapped the shore, and the humming of the summer insects, and the soft, rustling calls of the singing birds. Only gradually did she come to recognize the pungent odor of pine mingling with the more pleasing musky scent of her lover. The sun was bright and warmed them, but the trees gave them a sense of privacy that was invaded only by the gentle breezes.

After a while Robin rolled onto her stomach, cupping her chin in her hands. Her eyes grew bright and sparkling, but Nick did not notice. His own eyes were focused on the smooth length of her back as he caressed her gently.

"Nicholas?"

"Hmm?" His hand smoothed past her waist to rest in the small of her back. His voice echoed his distraction.

"Marriage is a very serious step."

Nick's hand stilled for a moment, then began a carefully executed trail up her spine. He was not distracted now and knew from the tone of her voice and the flirtatious glitter in Robin's eyes that she was about to say something outrageous.

"Hmm." This time his utterance was noncommittal.

Robin's attempt at nonchalance was not entirely successful, for Nick's fingers had found a particularly sensitive area between her shoulder blades. "I—unh." Taking a deep breath, she turned to him, twining her arms around his waist. When he gave a husky groan of longing, Robin laughed audaciously. "I think we need more practice, Nick."

"Minx!" Her sweater was pulled roughly over her head. Although the fingers that drew her cinnamon-colored hair from beneath it were gentle and tender, the voice was not. "Get dressed, Snow Queen. If we're to do any more practicing, I want to do it with my wedding ring on your finger."

Laughing, Robin scrambled into her clothing before lying back to watch Nick finish dressing. "I was right. You do have too many clothes. Look how long it's taking you to dress." Her eyes sparkled as Nick bent down to gather her into his arms again, but his expression was so gravely serious that Robin felt a momentary flutter of alarm.

"Robin, can you ever forgive me for leaving? It wasn't that I didn't love you—never think that—for I love you more than life itself. But I knew that I didn't deserve you—"

"True!" Robin shot back quickly. "But I'll have you know that I was very good last year and I'm not going to let anyone take my Christmas present away again. I fell madly in love with a man and I've made him mine—twice! Oh, no, Nicholas Armstrong, you may not deserve me, but I certainly deserve you. What's mine I keep." She laughed up at him, her jade eyes snapping audaciously. "Now, didn't you mention something about a license burning a hole in your pocket?"

"Mmm." Nick nibbled a path from her ear to the corner of her mouth. "Seems to me I did. Do you have a white dress?"

"White lace over jade silk. I've been saving it . . . just in case you came back."

"The whole outfit?" His eyes darkened dramatically.

"Mmm." Robin acknowledged, more interested in kissing his jaw than in the contents of her wardrobe.

Nick pulled her hastily to her feet. When she protested, he laughed. "Mrs. Armstrong, I can't wait to see you in all that sexy lace and satin. Can you be ready in an hour?"

Robin stood enthralled, her expression rapt. "Say it again, Nick."

"What?" he teased.

"My name."

"Snow Queen."

"No."

"Robin?"

She shook her head.

"Mrs. Armstrong?"

"Yes! Oh, yes! I love you Nicholas Armstrong."

Nicholas gathered her close. His voice was rough with emotion. "I love you too, Robin. I love you too."

Candlelight Ecstasy Romances™